PRAISE FOR SUSAN HATLER

"I have always loved Susan Hatler's romances... but this one goes to another level."
— Marsha @ Keeper Bookshelf on The Christmas Compromise

"Ms. Hatler has a way of writing witty dialogue that makes you laugh-out-loud throughout her stories."
— Night Owl Reviews

"I couldn't help but smile and laugh at the antics that Ben and Sarah go through. I'm so excited for this whole series!"
— Katie's Clean Book Collection re The Wedding Charm

"The Friendliest Festival is a wonderful and perfect release to a stressful or crazy day."
— Cafè of Dreams Book Reviews

"Susan Hatler's books always give me butterflies and swoony feelings with flirty banter and fun characters."
— Getting Your Read On Reviews

"Susan Hatler is the best at clean romcom and this one is at the top of my favorite list."
— YeahOrNeighReviews on Million Dollar Date

TITLES BY SUSAN HATLER

Blue Moon Bay Series
The Second Chance Inn
The Sisterhood Promise
The Wishing Star
The Friendly Cottage
The Christmas Cabin
The Oopsie Island
The Wedding Boutique
The Holiday Shoppe

Christmas Mountain Romance Series
The Christmas Compromise
'Twas the Kiss Before Christmas
A Sugar Plum Christmas
Fake Husband for Christmas
The Christmas Competition
A Gingerbread Christmas

The Wedding Whisperer Series
The Wedding Charm
The Wedding Connection
My Wedding Date
The Wedding Bet
The Wedding Promise

TITLES BY SUSAN HATLER

Better Date than Never Series
Love at First Date
Truth or Date
My Last Blind Date
Save the Date
A Twist of Date
License to Date
Driven to Date
Up to Date
Déjà Date
Date and Dash

Do-Over Date Series
Million Dollar Date
The Double Date Disaster
The Date Next Door
Date to the Rescue
The Dashing Date
Once Upon a Date
The Island Date
One Fine Date
The Date Mistake
The Decadent Date

TITLES BY SUSAN HATLER

Montana Dreams Series
The Friendliest Festival
The Delightful Dinner
The Brightest Boutique
The Memorable Mountain
The Welcoming Wedding
The Happiest Hike
The Sweetest Surprise
The Comforting Christmas

Young Adult Novels
See Me
The Crush Dilemma
Shaken

A SUGAR PLUM CHRISTMAS

SUSAN HATLER

A Sugar Plum Christmas
Copyright © 2020 by Susan Hatler

All rights reserved. Without limiting the rights under copyright reserved above, no part of this publication may be reproduced, stored in or introduced into a retrieval system, or transmitted, in any form, or by any means (electronic, mechanical, photocopying, recording, or otherwise) without the prior written permission of the copyright owner of this book. This is a work of fiction. Names, characters, places, brands, media, and incidents are either the product of the author's imagination or are used fictitiously.

ISBN: 9798579764737

Cover Design by Elaina Lee, For The Muse Design
www.forthemusedesign.com

** To receive a FREE BOOK , sign up for
Susan's Newsletter:
susanhatler.com/newsletter **

A SUGAR PLUM CHRISTMAS

SUSAN HATLER

DEDICATION

For you, dear reader.
May your holiday season,
be merry and bright.

CHAPTER ONE

I stepped out of the cab and into a winter wonderland that made me realize I should *not* have worn high heels to Christmas Mountain, Montana in December. Big mistake. This climate was no friend to my knock-off Christian Louboutin's, that was for sure.

As the tops of my feet started to freeze and the cabbie pulled my luggage from the trunk, I stood on the sidewalk looking at the expanse of holiday décor on Main Street and thought *wow*. This small town had clearly been named Christmas Mountain for a reason.

With only two weeks until Christmas, wreaths, ribbons and twinkling lights were aplenty, complimenting the white snow lining both sides of the sidewalk. I thanked my lucky stars I'd purchased snow boots and had stuffed them into my luggage before I left New York City, knowing that traveling this far into the wilderness—as my boss had called it—wouldn't warrant city attire. Unfortunately, I'd had no time to take my new boots out of the box yet or put together an appropriate outfit for this weather thanks to pulling an all-nighter at work (again).

What else could I do? I'd pitched a new concept for *Fourteen Days Till Forever* that had led me here to check out Christmas Mountain for a potential season shoot. The first three seasons of our reality dating show had taken place in Bora Bora, St. Barts and The Big Island of Hawaii. The show had been a huge hit so far with everyone and their mothers following our three happily married couples on social media. As producer of this uber popular show, I made a pitch to the executive producer to do something fresh for season four: small town America and snow.

Tons of ideas hit me last night and I couldn't sleep until every last idea to boost ratings was down on paper. The last guy I'd dated had dumped me saying I was a workaholic—as if that were a bad thing. Work meant security, which was something I'd never had growing up. At twenty-eight years old, I still longed for a permanent place to call home and if I pulled this new idea off then I'd finally have it.

So, I'd be spending the next two weeks here in Christmas Mountain doing research for the show. If my location gets approved then I'd be looking at a substantial bonus. Did I care that I'd have to work over the holidays? Kind of a bummer, but it wasn't like I had a family to visit. A tinge of sadness pierced my heart at that sad fact. But I forced myself to focus on getting this bonus and buying my own apartment.

I turned to ask the cab driver where I could find the best coffee in town before heading to the Sugar Plum Inn for check-in, but as I leaned down to peer through the open passenger window he pulled away with a cheery 'have a nice day'.

"I'll have a nice day when I can get to the inn and warm my feet," I said, looking around. "But first things first . . ." I

A Sugar Plum Christmas

needed caffeine before I dozed off right here on the sidewalk.

"Do you need help, dear?" a woman asked, giving me a puzzled look before noticing the luggage at my feet. "I'm Addie Wilcox," she said, holding out her hand.

"Lacey Lane," I said, taking her gloved hand in mine. "Nice to meet you."

"Are you looking for somewhere to stay?" she asked.

I shook my head, surprised at her friendliness. "Just an espresso."

She nodded. "You want Jingle Bells Bakery. Their coffee is excellent, but, more importantly, you can also get one of their famous cinnamon rolls."

My tummy rumbled. I'd eaten the pretzels the airline handed out but nothing else for lunch. "A cinnamon roll sounds delicious right now."

"The rolls from Jingle Bells Bakery are simply to die for. You'll love them. I'd walk you there myself but I'm late for a hair appointment at the C.M. Salon."

"No problem." I held my palms up then put them together in the prayer position. "You've already been most helpful. Long flight. Need the caffeine boost."

She smiled and then tilted her head. "You in town for pleasure?"

"Business," I said, taking hold of my suitcase handle.

"What kind of work do you do?" she asked, blinking at me intently. "If you don't mind my asking..."

"I'm in the entertainment business."

"Magazine?" she prodded, raising her eyebrows.

Hmm... This Addie Wilcox lady seemed like quite the busybody. But, a harmless busybody. "I'm a producer for *Fourteen Days Till Forever*, the—"

"Reality dating show," she exclaimed, with a loud squeal. "That is my favorite TV show. I never miss an episode."

I smiled. "We love to hear that."

"I have a question for you, Lacey." She leaned toward me, putting a hand on my arm. "Can you tell me if Gabrielle really dismissed Jeremy in episode seven last season because of his past? I never got the feeling she was telling the truth."

Ha! That's because Jeremy had been planted for the drama aspect and had never been a real bachelor candidate.

"I heard her say that, same as you," I said, truthfully, while keeping our show's secret to myself.

"Mmm . . ." She tapped her finger to her cheek just as her cell went off in her purse. "That's my alarm. I'm really late now. May I ask where you're staying, Lacey?"

"The Sugar Plum Inn," I said.

She nodded. "Randall and Betty Curtis's place. You'll love it."

"Good to know," I said, as she turned away from me with a wave. "Thanks again."

She nodded. "Bye-bye now!"

I pulled a recorder from my purse and spoke into the microphone. "Two minutes in Christmas Mountain and I've already met one of the townspeople. Super friendly, small town feel. Addie Wilcox enthused about the show and recommended Jingle Bells Bakery for coffee and cinnamon rolls. Sugar and caffeine are just what I need right now and just what our contestants will need during shooting. This is going to work," I said, keeping a positive attitude while slipping the recorder back into my purse and heading toward the cheerful looking awning with the big gold bells on either side of its business sign.

"This is a quaint little town, tucked away in the Rockies. The

viewers will love it," I had enthused when I'd pitched the idea to my boss, Melvin Pennington. My friend Carol Bennett had moved here last year, which was how this little mountain town had appeared on my radar.

I pulled the handle of my black bought-on-sale suitcase as I strode in the direction of the shops, but realized pretty quickly that the wheels on the bottom of the case were built for city streets and not the icy, snowy streets of Montana.

Grunting, I pondered having to carry the bag as I struggled with the weight from all my various electrical items nestled inside: flat iron (for when I wanted to look businesslike), my curling iron (for when I wanted to look cute), my hairdryer (because I didn't want to freeze by going outside with wet hair) and my laptop, my tablet, my spare tablet, and the array of chargers and cables that went with them all. Maybe I'd overpacked a little, but it's better to be prepared.

At the other end of Main Street, I spotted a magnificent mountain jutting up and providing a breathtaking backdrop. The mountain top was laden with pristine white snow, making it look like an iced cake with dark lower levels resembling a rich chocolate sponge. Small houses (at least they looked small from where I was standing) dotted the mountain. I thought about how peaceful it must be to live up there, looking down on the town. Strings of cables zigzagged above the ribbon of road, dangling multi-colored lights. I couldn't wait for dusk to fall to see them light up like a glowing rainbow connecting both sides of the road.

As I walked along the sidewalk, I marveled at the store names, and the little girl inside me couldn't help but get excited that this was definitely the place to shoot next season. I spotted Jingle Bells Bakery, The Sleigh Cafe, and a furniture store named Parker's, which appeared to share the same retail space as a beauty salon—what a random concept. I smiled, thinking it was all so quaint that the contestants on the show couldn't help but fall in love, both with the town and with each other. With this new location, season four would be the biggest hit yet!

As I wandered along, scene ideas popped into my head. I imagined contestants laughing as they threw snowballs at each other, and couples strolling arm in arm along the festively lit street as they 'oohed' and 'aahed' at the charming stores. It would be all woolly hats and mittens, with the woman taking her scarf off to wrap around a newly-built snowman's neck, and her date taking his scarf off and wrapping it around her neck so she would stay warm as he tenderly kissed the tip of her nose...

Ding-ding! Ding-ding! Ding-ding!

I shook my head, visions of the imagined show scene evaporating as I came out of my fog and realized my phone was ringing. I pulled one of my gloves off with my teeth before fishing around in my pocket to find my cell. I glanced at the screen, which read: MELVIN

I tapped on the ANSWER button and greeted my boss, "Hi, Mel. How are you?"

"Depends. How's it going there?"

I grinned. "It's perfect. You should see it."

"Not my scene. Give me the sun, sea, and sangria any day. You can keep the snow for the contestants. When it airs, I'll watch from the deck of my yacht." He let out a croaky laugh, the result of too many cigars and expensive whiskeys.

"That works," I said, feeling a little disappointed he wouldn't come to the shooting if the idea gets approved. Then again, Mel could be a bit intense. Maybe it would be better if he steered clear. But I owed him a lot for taking a chance on an unknown like me three years ago and I didn't want to disappoint him.

"Mel, I'm going to phone you back on a video call. You need to see this place. It's like Christmas come to life. I'm heading to get coffee at a place called Jingle Bells Bakery. For real," I said, before ending the call.

I redialed Mel's number and a moment later his face filled the screen as he answered.

"Okay, Mel. I'm going to turn you around so you can see Main Street and the town square. Are you ready for this?" I pressed the flip screen button so Mel could see the view as I walked, dragging my suitcase with one hand while holding the phone up to show my boss the sights. "This town is the epitome of Christmas. The viewers are going to love it."

"Prancer's Pancake House?" he asked, letting out a throaty chuckle. "The ratings are going to soar!"

I laughed. "A lot of the shops seem to be named after Christmas in one way or another. I saw a sign for Silver Bell's Luxury Tours as I got out of the cab. When I check into the inn, I'll have to ask about it."

"Find the cutesiest places you can, Lacey," he said, pausing and audibly puffing on his cigar. "The more fanciful the town is, the more viewers will tune in, and it's all about the ratings."

"Right, the ratings," I said, knowing that was our business priority. But, finding the perfect location for contestants to fall in love was equally important to me. "I'm going to go into Jingle Bells Bakery now. I'll call you lat—" My voice cut off as my shoulder suddenly rammed into a metal ladder in my way and the phone flew out of my hand.

Beside me, I heard a loud *thump* followed by a grunt, and a flash of denim passed the corner of my eye. I gasped in horror as my brain processed what just happened: A man had been up on the ladder. I'd knocked into the ladder (which seemed way too far out on the sidewalk in my opinion). The man fell into a giant pot of poinsettias. Oops.

"Oh, no!" I exclaimed, holding my hand out to the man who was sprawled backward with his head against the window of the bakery. The producer in me couldn't help but make a mental note that this would make an intriguing scene between two contestants. "Here, let me help you up."

"You could've just said hello," the man said, before taking my hand and standing up. A generous amount of snow covered his shoulders and beanie hat. Perhaps my fault?

"I'm sorry, I just—" I lifted my lashes to explain my clumsiness and stopped short when I gazed into deep blue eyes that seemed to peer right into my soul. A zap zipped through my belly. Oh, my. I bit my bottom lip, taking in the rest of the man's handsome face, noting the blond hair peeking out from beneath a navy-blue beanie hat. "Um, yeah, sorry."

"New to town?" he asked.

"Visiting," I said, realizing his hand still held mine. Or was I holding his hand? Oh, great, *that* was the part I was focusing on when I'd almost killed the guy? "Are you all right?"

"Nothing seems broken," he said, the corners of his eyes crinkling. "I'm guessing you're from the city."

I tilted my head. "Why do you say that?"

"You were walking full speed while on a video call and—"

"Whoa, wait a minute." I blinked and then remembered I'd hung up on Mel. Er, either that or he was still on the line wherever my phone had landed. Argh! "My phone..."

I let go of the man's hand and scanned the sidewalk, but

my cell was nowhere in sight. Where had it gone? I'd been trying to impress my boss with a fabulous idea, not get fired due to my penchant for clumsiness. A dark-haired woman walked by on the sidewalk and gave me a sympathetic smile that said she'd seen the entire thing. Great. Ten minutes in town and I'd already made a spectacle. So *not* my intention.

"Here," the man (aka: my victim) said, brushing the snow off his shoulders and then holding his other hand out to me. "Found this in the hood of my jacket. Must be yours."

"Yes, thanks!" I exclaimed, my cheeks heating as I took the cell phone from him. "And, I am from the city, actually."

"No kidding," he said, the corners of his mouth twitching.

Wait, was he laughing at me? My eyebrows came together.

"Are you trying to infer that people from the city make more mistakes than people from a small town?" I asked, raising an eyebrow and waiting for him to look remorseful for that smirky look on his handsome face. "I did apologize."

"You don't look overly sorry with that scowl," he said, which annoyed me—mostly because he was probably right.

"Well, you didn't accept my apology, did you?"

The corner of his mouth lifted. "New York City. Am I right?"

My mouth dropped open. "What are you implying?"

"Just asking because—"

"Because you're judgmental?" I asked, straightening my coat and then lifting the handle of my luggage for the umpteenth time since I'd arrived. "Look, just because I was on the phone and just because I was walking fast doesn't mean I'm from New York City."

"I just—"

"Fine, I'm from New York City," I said, throwing my

hands up because there was no getting around that fact. "I may have knocked into your ladder by accident. An accident, by the way, is what you call it when something is *not* done on purpose, you know. But I do feel bad for knocking you into the pot of poinsettias, so, again, I'm sorry."

He slipped his hands in his front pockets. "I can tell."

My eyes flared. Why couldn't he just accept my apology like a nice human being? Why did he insist on teasing me while looking so hot?

"Look, I'm tired," I said, holding my palm up. "I thought I needed a coffee, but now I just want to rest. Laugh at my obvious remorse all you want, but would you please tell me where I might find the Sugar Plum Inn?"

"The Sugar Plum Inn is right over there," he said, leaning against the ladder with an almost imperceptible nod of his head. "Take a left at the town square and it's up the street past The Falls."

"Thank you very much," I said, giving him a firm nod as I squeezed the handle of my luggage and turned to head up the street. "Again, I'm sorry."

"Hang on," he said, still not accepting my umpteenth apology. Instead, he surprised me by coming up beside me and taking hold of my luggage. "I'm heading that way, actually."

"You're staying at the inn, too?" I asked, noting that the thought made me a little excited.

He shook his head. "Visiting my parents."

"Your parents?" I asked, blinking.

"They own the Sugar Plum Inn," he said, giving me a sideways glance. "And . . . I work there."

"You do?" I asked, blinking.

"Jacob Curtis," he said, holding his hand out.

"Lacey Lane," I said, taking his hand, and a little rush rolled through me at the feel of his hand in mine again.

"Yeah, I know. From New York City. We've been expecting you."

My cheeks heated. So *that* was why he'd asked if I was from New York City. He'd known because I was a guest at the inn, not because he was making fun of me for walking fast and talking on the phone. I felt like such an airhead . . . wait, my phone!

I turned the cell phone over in my other hand, pressed the flip button and saw Mel's face gazing back at me. I stared at the screen as I walked up the street. "Mel, you're still there?"

"Yes," he said, blowing cigar smoke into the lens. "And if that little exchange was any indication of the conflict and tension we'll be shooting in that town then this season is going to be a huge hit. Get to work, Lacey. I'm counting on you."

"Yes, sir," I said, hanging up the phone.

"Welcome to Christmas Mountain," Jacob said, as we approached the front door of the charming inn. "Hope you enjoy your stay."

"Thanks," I said, turning to him. The corners of his mouth curved upward and my belly did a cartwheel that made me lightheaded. What was going on?

Okay, yes, Jacob Curtis was attractive. One couldn't have eyes and not admit that fact. But I was *not* here to swoon over the innkeeper's son. He may work at the inn where I'd be staying for the next two weeks as I did my research for the show, but that didn't mean I would let him distract me. I was here to do my job, and nothing else. End of story.

CHAPTER TWO

As Jacob Curtis stood behind the reception desk, checking me into the Sugar Plum Inn, I felt unsettled and couldn't figure out why. Maybe it was because I'd apologized a gazillion times for knocking him off the ladder and not once had he accepted my apology. I mean, it wasn't like I go around knocking tall, hot guys with amazing eyes off ladders for fun.

Although that prospect wasn't without appeal...

"Look, I'm really sorry I knocked you into that pot of poinsettias," I blurted, as if apologizing to Jacob had become a habit I couldn't resist. "I was just so excited by the uniqueness of this charming town. I mean, how could I not be? It's beyond festive."

"Festive is what we do best here," Jacob said, once again not accepting my apology. Instead, he looked me up and down with a curious brow. Not in a creepy-guy-in-a-bar kind of way, but more in a surprised-at-my-outfit kind of way.

I glanced down at my pink silk blouse, black slacks, and high heels. I'd change into warmer clothes once I got to my room. At least my feet were starting to tingle since we'd come in from the freezing cold. Progress.

"How long are you staying at the inn?" he asked, typing into the computer behind the desk.

"Are you trying to get rid of me already?" I joked, trying to tease him like he'd done to me.

Instead of laughing, he looked confused. "Why would I try to get rid of you?"

"I don't know . . ." Wishing I hadn't tried to make a joke with someone who clearly didn't like me, I glanced around the room. There was a cozy seating area with thick leather couches and a floor-to-ceiling stone fireplace. Guests seated on the sofas were dressed in jeans, sweaters and boots. They looked warm, too. Must be nice.

"You've reserved your room for two weeks, until December twenty-third. Is that correct?"

"Yes," I said, glancing over at Jacob as he typed at his keyboard. His blue eyes were fixed on the screen and his mouth twitched in an adorable way as he worked. He'd make an interesting contestant on the show if we decided to hold local auditions. "So, what were you doing up on that ladder before I knocked into you?" I asked.

"Changing a light bulb for a friend." He reached into the front pocket of his blue and black flannel shirt and winced, before pulling out a broken green lightbulb. I noticed a thin red scratch on his wrist.

"Is that from the fall? I'm so sorry!" I blurted, feeling terrible.

He reached inside his pocket again and pulled out remnants of a lightbulb. "Guess I won't be using this anymore."

I rummaged in my purse and then pulled out a packet of tissues. "Here, you can wrap the shards in this for safety."

"Thanks." His finger brushed mine as he accepted the tissue I held out.

Tingles warmed my skin where he'd touched and I felt butterflies dance in my belly. Did I have a crush on the innkeeper's son? That would so not be a good idea. I clasped my hands together, trying to wipe away the effect he seemed to have on me.

He nodded at my suitcase. "What brings a city girl to Christmas Mountain?"

I didn't know whether to be offended or flattered that he was asking, but was it hot in here? I unbuttoned my coat, draping it over my arm.

"I'm a producer on *Fourteen Days Till Forever*," I said, waiting expectantly for an excited reaction similar to the one Addie Wilcox had earlier. Jacob's expression remained impassive. "It's a reality dating show?" I prodded.

He shook his head. "I don't watch much TV."

Why didn't that surprise me? "Okay, well, it's a show where we arrange for people with common interests to go on fabulous dates for two weeks in a beautiful setting, and hope that they fall in love."

"And that's it?"

That stung a little, I had to admit.

"Well, obviously there's more to the show than that, but . . . that's the gist."

Jacob continued typing at the keyboard. "What happened to two people meeting and spending time together the old-fashioned way?"

I was taken aback. In New York, the men I'd dated were impressed that I produced a hit show. And they didn't talk about old-fashioned romance at all. In fact, the last guy I'd dated had been all about expediting things. He'd even had his assistant call to schedule our dates and he'd broken up with me via text message.

"Well . . ." I was stuck for words, a first for me. "Life is busy, you know? Everyone is always working and it's hard to meet new people."

"You and I met, didn't we?"

"We're not dating," I pointed out, noting the argument didn't feel like a win.

"Maybe some people are too busy to meet other people. They're too busy to *notice*."

His challenge threw me and I didn't know how to answer. So, I did what I always did when I get nervous . . . I started talking way too much.

"Anyway, we chose, well, actually, I chose to look into Christmas Mountain because a small mountain town sounds romantic. My friend, Carol Bennett, you might know her? She owns Rudolph's Reads and moved here last year. When she posted photos of this town online, I thought it would be the perfect place to film the next season of *Fourteen Days Till Forever*. I mean, what location could be more picturesque than this?" I swept my arm around the lobby and seating area of the inn. "We're bound to form a successful relationship here."

"Sure, this is a great town for romance. With the local events, including Silver Bells Luxury Tours, there is plenty of magic that happens here." Jacob raised a shoulder. "But what happens when the contestants on your show go back to their normal lives in their normal towns, and there's no snow, no Christmas lights and no Christmas Mountain? What then?"

"Are you suggesting that our couples can only be in love while on the show?" I asked, my mouth dropping open that he'd suggested such a thing. "For your information, our winning couple from last season already exchanged wedding vows and they have three million followers on social media."

His blue eyes peered up at me. "What do social media followers have to do with their relationship?"

"Their love is inspiring to others," I said, using a tone that showed the reason was obvious.

"All of the couples make it once the cameras are off?" he asked.

I sighed, wishing I could disagree with him for some reason. "Not all of them make it."

He nodded. "You don't say."

"Maybe some people are too annoying to make a relationship work," I pondered, hoping he would get my meaning. My retort was a tad obnoxious, but he was insulting my work, which I took a lot of pride in. "Anyway, for the next two weeks I'll be taking a look around Christmas Mountain. But I have to say that so far I think the location is ideal."

"Here's the key to your room," he said, handing me a long bronze key that had a jeweled purple head in the shape of three sugar plums banded together.

"Thanks," I said, feeling annoyed that he didn't seem to think having the show here was a good idea. I took a few steps away from him and glanced out the massive window at the front of the inn. The view faced the town with its twinkling lights and the majestic mountain jutting up behind it. I sucked in a deep breath. "Picture this, Jacob."

"What?" he asked, coming up beside me.

I gestured toward the line of shops on Main Street. "We film the couples in one of those cute little cafes. They sit across from each other and their eyes meet over two mugs of steaming hot cocoa."

He glanced over at me. "Cocoa?"

"Yes, everyone loves cocoa," I said, new ideas popping into my head. "And. . . I'll need to run it by my boss because of insurance and stuff, but we could have some kind of mini winter Olympics. I'm thinking skiing and snowboarding with lessons from a resident instructor from the ski resort," I said, looking over at him.

His blue eyes met mine. "Do you like to ski?"

"Me? I've never been."

"Maybe you should try it," he said.

"I'll take that to mean you like the idea," I said, giving him a coy side glance. "The lessons will be good for this town, including the inn," I said, turning back to the window, wanting to convince him that hosting the show here was a wonderful idea. "The show will bring a lot of business to this town, you know? It won't just be the contestants staying here, either. The whole production crew will need accommodations, too."

He made a noise. "Sounds crowded."

"Like a big party," I said, smiling at him and trying to spin his comment into something positive since I obviously hadn't won him over yet. Those blue eyes deepened, making my belly do a little flip, so I turned to look out the window again. "Filming the show here will be a big treat for the town and visitors alike. Do you know any ski instructors who wouldn't mind being on camera or would I have to bring them in from the city?" I asked.

Dead silence followed.

I opened my mouth as I turned to Jacob, but he wasn't there. What the . . . ?

I glanced around the room, but he was nowhere to be seen. Not only had he failed to see the light about my idea to film the show here, but he hadn't even finished listening to my pitch. My eyebrows came together. I'd been ghosted by a man I'd dated back in the city, but I'd never been *literally* ghosted by a guy standing beside me who had vanished into thin air.

Not that Jacob and I were dating . . . or that I wanted to go on a date with him.

With a sigh, I grabbed the handle of my suitcase and headed to my room. I *so* needed a nap to wipe Jacob out of my head. Unfortunately, once I'd plopped down on the bed with my head on the pillow, I could think of nothing but him.

CHAPTER THREE

After trying to nap for an hour, I finally gave up. I changed into winterwear, broke out my new boots and went downstairs. As I reached the bottom step, I saw the window where Jacob and I had stood together when he had suddenly disappeared. I still couldn't believe he'd ghosted me. Was he *that* opposed to filming a hit show in his town?

My eyebrows raised as I stepped down to the hardwood floor. It didn't matter what Jacob Curtis thought. I felt certain the show would do well here and it would bring a lot of attention and business to this charming town. Plus, Jacob's response had to be an anomaly. Addie Wilcox had certainly been excited about the possibility.

Warmth from the fireplace and a hint of cinnamon hit me as I entered the seating area. Above the fireplace sat a red and green garland with gold balls threaded together. Higher up, above the mantel, sat an old-fashioned cuckoo clock with a door above the clock face and a bell underneath, flanked by two dolls—an old man and an old woman—who were poised with wooden mallets to presumably strike the bell as each hour passed. Framed pictures covered the mantel on either side of the clock. So sweet.

The walls to either side of the fireplace, were clad in pine, giving the whole room the feel of a cozy log cabin. I glanced at the reception desk where Jacob had checked me in earlier which was against the far wall by the front door, but a woman sat there now. A small Christmas tree stood on one end of the desk, but the main feature of the room that caught my attention was the enormous tree that took up one corner. The tree was decorated in the same colors as the garland but on a much grander scale, with luxurious, thick tinsel and twinkling lights that brought the tree to life as the colors danced.

A red rug covered most of the floor and I crossed over it as I walked toward the reception desk, admiring the tiny green holly leaves pattern swirling throughout. I approached the woman behind the desk, who looked about my age. Her blonde hair was pulled up into a high ponytail and she wore a red sweater with jeans. As I approached, she popped her head up from behind the desk and smiled at me.

"Hi! Welcome to the Sugar Plum Inn. You must be Lacey?"

"Yes," I said, wondering if she was the person I'd spoken with when I made my reservation. If so, she'd sounded much older on the phone. "And you're ... Mrs. Curtis?"

She laughed. "Well, I go by Ms. actually. You're probably thinking of my mom. I'm Ruby Curtis, Betty's daughter."

That made her Jacob's sister. Interesting.

I put my hand to my chest. "I'm sorry, I didn't realize ..."

"No big deal." Ruby waved away my apology. "How was your flight? And your trip from the airport? Mom said you're filming a TV show here? How exciting!"

"Hoping to film a TV show, but thanks. It is exciting," I said, thinking *this* was the reaction I'd been hoping for from everyone. "I'm looking forward to researching this town to see if it will work to film a season here. I love how everything seems to be sprinkled with Christmas."

"We are all about Christmas in this town." She smiled, leaned her elbows on the desk and put her chin in her hands. "Now, tell me the truth. Do you meet lots of celebrities?"

"No, just ordinary people. Well, until after they finish the show, anyway," I said, covering my mouth to stifle a yawn. "Then they're a celebrity in their own right."

"Where are my manners?" Ruby stood up and walked in front of the desk. "I shouldn't be pelting you with questions when you must be exhausted from traveling. Is there anything I can do to help you enjoy your stay?"

I opened my mouth to speak and then yawned again. "Actually... Do you know where I can get a coffee?"

"Of course! The kitchen. Follow me." Ruby led the way down a hallway beyond the stairs, with me following close behind as she explained that there was no elevator because her parents hadn't wanted to mess with the old-fashioned charm of the place. "Here we are..."

"This entire inn is lovely," I said, as we walked into the kitchen. The room was large with a dark butcherblock countertop island and slate-gray countertops throughout the rest of the kitchen. In the corner of the room by the enormous floor to ceiling window was a Christmas tree, decorated the same way as the one in the sitting area by the lobby.

"This tree is bigger than the one in my apartment," I said, thinking I might need to upgrade from the little artificial tree I pulled out year after year.

Ruby nodded. "In my family's book, the bigger the tree the better it is."

I laughed. "I'm starting to see that."

She poured coffee grounds into the espresso machine and tamped them down. "Your booking noted that you'd like a tour of the town. I can do that now if you'd like, before it gets dark? Or we could leave it until tomorrow if you're tired."

I thought for a moment. I *was* tired and the bed still sounded inviting, with its plump pillows and deep red covers. On the other hand, I wanted to see the town to scout out some places for filming. I had promised Mel some photos by the end of the day.

"If you have time for a tour now then that would be great. This jolt of caffeine will give me my second wind, thanks," I said, inhaling the delicious aroma of espresso as the rich brown liquid dripped into a beige mug. "If you're too busy, though, I could go and have a look around by myself and—"

"You can't do that! You're a city girl. There have been reports of bears coming down from the mountain and into the town, and if you're not with a local then..."

My eyes widened. "You're joking, right?"

"Yes, of course I'm joking," she said, giving a little laugh. "Just a little mountain girl humor. But in all seriousness, I'll give you the grand tour of the town and—"

Brring! Brring! Brring!

Ruby's cell phone started ringing and she fished around in her jeans pocket for it, mouthing an apology as she handed me a coffee mug with frothed milk on top and moved toward the hall.

"Sorry about that," she said, returning with an apologetic look. "I'm not going to be able to give you that tour. I'm sorry, but one of my dogs has escaped and I need to find him."

"Oh, no! How many dogs do you have?"

Ruby shook her head. "He's not *my* dog exactly. I own Divine Doggie Spa and Training."

"Your own business?"

She nodded. "Ribbons has run off and this isn't his first time. I need to find him or the bear snack thing will be no joke."

"The dog's name is Ribbons?"

She nodded. "He's a two-year-old St. Bernard, who should have been named Houdini. He's always getting away from us and his owner, too. Luckily, everyone around town knows him so hopefully someone will grab him and hold him until I get there."

I took a sip of my latte and set the mug on the counter. "I'll help you track him down. Two sets of eyes are better than one."

"No, honestly, it's fine." She shook her head and held up her hands. "You're in town to see the sights and I've got this, really. So sweet of you to offer, though. If he's not in town then I'll jump on a snowmobile and head into the forest to search and it's only a one-seater."

"Snowmobile?" I asked.

She nodded. "I'm guessing you don't have much reason for riding a snowmobile in the city?"

I shook my head. "Not so much."

She laughed. "Welcome to Montana."

"Thanks, and good luck," I said, hoping she found the dog before it got dark. "We can do the tour tomorrow?"

She tapped on her cell phone screen. "Hang on a sec... yep, got an answer. You're still good for a tour today. My brother will show you around."

"Your brother?" I asked, those beautiful blue eyes popping into my head.

"I sent him a text letting him know I had an emergency and asking him to fill in for the tour. He'll be down in a sec."

I held my palms up. "No, that's okay. I can wait until tomorrow."

She waved a hand. "Don't be silly."

I stretched my arms high above my head and gave an exaggerated yawn. "Guess the coffee didn't work. I should take a nap. But thanks for the offer."

"Are you worried about troubling him?" Ruby asked, shaking her head. "You New Yorkers are too polite. Really, tours are part of our job at the inn. He'll be in deep trouble with my mom if he doesn't give you the tour."

Ah, so that was why he'd agreed to show me around. Threat of punishment.

I backed toward the exit. "No, really, Ruby. Thanks, but I'll see you tom—"

"Here he is!" she exclaimed, walking over to Jacob as he entered the kitchen. She put an arm around him and squeezed. "Lacey, this is my brother, Jacob. He'll give you the grand tour of Christmas Mountain. Jacob, this is Lacey."

The corner of his mouth lifted. "We've met."

And there stood my *ghost*, looking handsome with his hair still damp from a shower. It's just my luck to get stuck on a tour with the one person in town who seemed to hate the possibility of us filming here. And the one person who made my legs go weak like they were doing right now.

"Um, yeah, we've met," I said, reaching onto the counter for support due to my sudden spaghetti legs. Given the ghosting earlier I decided to give him an easy way out so he wouldn't feel obligated to show me around. "Honestly, I can wait until tomorrow for the tour from you, Ruby. I'm sure Jacob has better things to do than show me around."

"Actually, I've cleared the rest of my day," he said.

I bit my bottom lip. "You did?"

"Yep. I'm all yours."

All mine? I hated that it was a proposition I didn't want to refuse.

CHAPTER FOUR

The kitchen at the Sugar Plum Inn drew a very awkward silence as I waffled between staring at my empty coffee mug, at the ceiling, and glancing between Ruby and Jacob. I really didn't want to make a big deal out of Jacob disappearing on me earlier. But it ranked right up there as one of my weirdest experiences ever.

Ruby gave Jacob an odd look. "How and when did you meet Lacey?"

Jacob locked his gaze on mine. "She knocked me off a ladder earlier. Sent me sprawling into a pot of cacti."

I sucked in a breath. "They were poinsettias..."

He shrugged. "Felt sharper."

Ruby laughed. "Sounds like Jacob's ego took a fair beating, too."

"Thanks, sis," he said, his voice dripping with sarcasm. "Don't you have an emergency to get to?"

"Ribbons!" she exclaimed, putting her hands to both cheeks before shuffling her feet toward the exit. "You're lucky I have to go. But we'll return to this conversation later."

"Can't wait," Jacob said.

"Be safe, you two," Ruby called over her shoulder before she ran out the door, leaving me alone with the man who had ghosted me.

I turned to Jacob. "So . . ."

"So," he said, the corners of his mouth twitching.

"Are you serious about giving me the grand tour?" I asked.

"It's what you ordered."

"Part of your job. Right. I get it."

His eyebrow rose. "Is there a problem?"

Yes. "No."

I went to brush past him, but he put a hand on my arm stopping me.

"What?" I asked, turning toward him. I lifted my lashes to find his gaze locked on mine from only a step away. My breath caught in my throat. As we stared at each other, the air between us thickened until it became almost palpable. His blue eyes peered into mine as the seconds ticked by in silence. I felt the strong and sudden urge to close the distance between us and kiss him.

His eyes darkened. "Look, I'm sorry for disappearing earlier."

"I understand," I said, giving a little shrug. "You hate the idea of us filming here."

"That's not why I left," he said, his tone low as he squeezed my arm.

I blinked. "Why did you then?"

He paused a long moment. "Something I had to deal with."

I waited for him to explain further, but he didn't.

"Apology accepted," I said, deciding I couldn't stay this

close to him without making a move and that would so *not* be a good idea. "We should go."

He nodded, looking down at my arm before letting me go. "After you."

"Thanks," I said, wishing I didn't miss the feel of his hand on my arm. I reminded myself I needed to stay focused and not let the innkeeper's attractive son distract me from my job. As I turned away from him, I caught the heady scent of his earthy soap and inhaled deeply. Oh, yum.

Jacob came up beside me, giving me a side-glance. "Everything all right?"

"Of course," I said, clearing my throat as we walked down the hall toward the living room and lobby. "Just thinking about work."

He made a little noise. "You do that a lot."

I nodded. "Well, it is why I'm here."

"Touché."

"He acquiesces for once." I let out a little laugh, feeling some of the tension between us dissipate.

"Anything in particular you're interested in seeing first?" he asked, his arm brushing mine as he moved toward the front door ahead of me to open it.

"Maybe you can show me some of the prettier places around town," I said, walking past him and breathing in that earthy soap. "You know, the kind of thing viewers will swoon over."

He raised his eyebrows. "I have no idea what viewers would *swoon* over," he said, using his fingers to make air quotes around the word "swoon."

I rolled my eyes, tightening my jacket around me as we stepped outside into the cold air. "Just show me the prettiest sights."

"All of Christmas Mountain is pretty. Even more so

now."

My heart skipped a beat. What did he mean by that? I swallowed. "Prettier? How so?"

"The snow," he said, his tone deadpan but there was a twinkle in his eye.

My cheeks heated. "Oh, right. Of course."

"Let's take a walk. If you see something you like then I'll give you a little bit of background about it, show you around inside, that kind of thing. Sound like a plan?" he asked, as we walked past the town square.

"Yes, that works," I said, glancing over at him as he zipped his jacket all the way up, making him look cozy enough to snuggle. "Thanks, Jacob."

"My pleasure," he said, giving me a wink.

Needing a distraction from him, I lifted my cell phone camera and took a couple of shots of Main Street with the spectacular view of the mountain behind it. Christmas Mountain would definitely make a nice backdrop for filming. So majestic and breathtaking.

"Okay, well . . ." I looked around, feeling like a kid in a candy store, because there were so many choices to check out: the toy store, the bakery, the adventure store...

"What's your pleasure?" he asked, as if reading my mind.

I pointed to the salon/furniture store I'd seen when I arrived. "How about the C.M. Salon slash Parker's Furniture?"

He raised his eyebrows. "That's what you want to know about?"

"The place is an anomaly." I nodded, taking in the brightly lit Christmas tree in the window along with the woman who was adjusting the lights and tinsel around it. "I mean, how did a hair salon end up with a furniture store attached to it?"

We strolled down Main Street as Jacob filled me in on the lease mix-up two years ago that caused both businesses to move into the same location at the same time while the landlord was out of the country on an African safari.

I lifted my camera and took another photo. "How does something like that happen?"

"Beats me. But Morgan . . ." He waved to the woman inside the window, who smiled and waved back. "She and Dallas, the furniture maker, each refused to back out of their lease agreements. They set up their businesses side by side, each thinking the other would give in first and find another location."

"And neither of them did?" I ventured.

He smiled. "Nope, they fell in love instead."

My heart skipped a beat. "For real?"

He nodded. "They're still going strong."

I clapped. "I *knew* this town was perfect for the show."

His smile faded. "What would you like to see next?"

"Is it okay if we take a look at Jingle Bells Bakery? I met a woman named Addie Wilcox today, who told me about their famous cinnamon rolls."

"Addie has good taste."

"You know Addie?"

"Of course. Small town, remember?"

I shook my head. "Do you know everyone who lives here?"

He shrugged. "Not everyone. But I went to school with Addie's daughter, Macy."

"An old-girlfriend?" I blurted, feeling irrationally jealous.

He glanced over at me, shaking his head. "No, she actually dated Morgan's older brother back in high school."

"The hair salon owner's brother?" I asked, feeling oddly happy by this news. "Wow. Small town."

We set off across the street with Jacob taking long strides. Luckily, my new boots seemed to be working well on the icy pavement as I hurried to keep up with him.

"Sorry, I forgot you're a city gal," he said, his tone teasing as he slowed his pace. "Here in Montana we're used to walking on the white stuff."

"We get snow in New York." I caught up to him, glancing at his arm and thinking that if I started to fall then I could grab on to that strong bicep. I wondered if Jacob would like that idea as much as I did.

Stop, Lacey. *Stop*. Why was I fantasizing about my tour guide? It had clearly been way too long since I'd had a decent date. That must be what was going on.

When we arrived at the bakery, I looked through the window and saw it was packed inside. Jacob suggested we come back another day when it was less busy. I nodded in agreement, but then a customer opened the door and came out, the scent of cinnamon reaching my nose and making my tummy rumble. Yum.

"It's a shame we can't package that scent during filming," I mused.

Jacob shook his head. "Dare I ask?"

"Wouldn't it be cool if we could send that cinnamon scent through the TV during the show to give the viewers another sense of this place. They would *love* it. It's so . . . Christmassy."

He gave me a side-glance. "A manufactured scent wouldn't come close to the real thing."

"*Bah humbug*," I said, scrunching up my nose.

"You're comparing me to Ebenezer Scrooge?" he asked, the corner of his mouth lifting.

"If the grouch fits," I joked, giving him a side-glance.

"I see how it is," he said, smiling at me.

"Imagine this scene, Jacob," I said, holding my hands up. "A woman comes out of the bakery with a paper bag full of pastries. She pulls a pastry out, bites into it and, I don't know, drops of applesauce spill onto her chin. Her date nudges the sauce away with his finger, gazes into her eyes and then kisses her as the snow falls around them."

Swoon. I smiled, feeling quite proud of that little scene I'd created.

"Ouch," Jacob said.

I thought he might've hurt himself, but I turned to find him leaning against the wall of the bakery with an amused look on his face. "Ouch?" I asked.

He nodded. "Yup. Applesauce can get mighty hot in those pastries."

I gave him an incredulous look. "That's where your mind goes?"

He shrugged. "Maybe the man can take the woman to the emergency room for burn ointment."

"Congratulations on ruining my scene," I said, wondering why I'd unwittingly pictured him as the hero and me as the heroine in that little scenario. Yeah, right.

He pushed away from the wall and pointed down the street. "Let's move on."

I looked at him. "I can't wait."

"I'll take you to where the good stuff happens." He stopped for a car to pass and then put a hand on the small of my back as we crossed a road over to a plain building. The windows were full of photos, mostly black and white but some in faded color. Not charming like Main Street.

"What is this? The county jail?"

"You'll see." He smiled and pushed open the door. "After

you."

I went inside, taking in the dark interior, paneled walls and green carpet. The wooden desks looked beat-up and there was a long walnut table in the conference room. This so did *not* look like a good place for a romantic scene.

"Is this a museum?" I asked, wrinkling my nose at the dusty smell.

"Not exactly, although some people do call me an old dinosaur," came a female voice.

I jumped back, thrusting a hand to my chest.

The woman who came toward me wore a red and yellow shirt and held her hand out. "I'm Doreen Halifax. Welcome to The Christmas Mountain Herald."

"Lacey Lane," I said, shaking her hand and wondering why Jacob thought the local newspaper would be a good place to shoot a scene. Kind of drab here, unfortunately.

Jacob shook her hand next. "Sorry for the intrusion, Doreen. I wanted to let Lacey come to the one place you can find out anything and everything about Christmas Mountain."

Doreen winked at him. "Jacob is right, Lacey. Nothing happens in this town without us hearing about it."

"Is that so?" I asked, my curiosity piqued.

Jacob explained about my show and a look of bemusement crossed the woman's face.

"A reality TV show in Christmas Mountain? I'm not sure about that," Doreen said, lifting a pencil and a pad of paper.

Great. Another Debbie Downer about filming here. Just what I didn't need.

"Right now, we're just considering filming the next season here," I said, wanting to make sure she didn't print an announcement by mistake. "Nothing has been confirmed."

"So, you're not sure if this town is good enough for you?" Doreen asked.

"No, it's not that at all," I said, trying to think fast on my feet. I certainly didn't want to insult the town or anyone in it. Yikes! "I'm just here to gather information on this wonderful town to submit the location for approval."

"Could be disruptive to the town having streets blocked off for filming," Doreen said.

"Do you watch *Fourteen Days Till Forever?*" I asked, crossing my fingers that she might be a fan and change her mind.

"Don't turn on the television much," she said, just as the phone on her desk rang. She stepped in that direction and lifted the receiver. "Good luck to you, Lacey."

"Thanks," I said, as she answered the phone.

"Ready to go?" Jacob asked, holding the door open.

Once outside I took a deep breath of fresh air. "Are you trying to get me in trouble?"

He shook his head. "Nope, I'm showing you the heart and soul of the town. If you want romance stories, Doreen has seen them all."

"I'd be hard pressed to find any romance in there. It smelled like cabbage."

Jacob chuckled. "Part of the charm. It's one of our oldest establishments."

"Believe me, I could tell it was aged."

He nudged me with his elbow. "Think of it as a town landmark."

"I need something that will pull in the viewers," I said, trying to put the Christmas Mountain Herald (and its smell) behind me. "Can we go to Prancer's Pancake House? Get a hot chocolate or something?"

"Sure," he said, his mouth curving into a knowing smile.

"What?" I asked.

"Not a thing," he said.

"Hmm..." I couldn't help wondering what he was thinking. That smile on his face told me something was up. I just hoped this next place would be better than the last.

* * *

Prancer's Pancake House was more than a block away from the smelly Herald office and sat close to the inn but on the other side of the Falls. As I stepped inside, the warmth wrapped around my shoulders like a comfy blanket. Laughter came from a group of people sitting at one table, and a loud but friendly debate was going on at another.

Christmas carols were playing through a speaker behind the counter and the smell of maple syrup was phenomenal. I checked out the menu board, my eyes moving past the waffles, pancakes, crepes, and a zillion toppings to go with them. It was Lauren's Luscious Latte that caught my eye. I could do with another shot of caffeine right about now.

I went to pull a chair out at the only vacant table, but Jacob kept walking so I followed him, wondering if there were more tables out back or something. My hopes were dashed when we entered the kitchen—a tiny, cramped space which was way too hot with my big puffy coat.

A woman about my age, who wore a reindeer-themed apron stepped toward us, wiping her hands on a cloth as she turned to Jacob.

He smiled at her. "Lauren, this is Lacey."

"Hi, Lacey," she said, shaking my hand warmly. "It's nice to meet you."

"You, too," I said, admiring her snowflake-painted fingernails.

"Oh," she said, turning her hand over to glance at her nails. "Lilly and I went to the C.M. salon to get our nails done."

"Lilly?" I asked.

"Another server here," she said, flicking her gaze back to Jacob. "The usual?"

"Yep," he said.

"Anything for you?" she asked, turning to me.

"I'd love a Lauren's Luscious Latte and a pancake," I said, noting the drink must've been named after her.

"Excellent choice," she said, giving me a wink.

"Thanks," I said, getting ready to leave the kitchen. But Jacob started chatting with Lauren, who didn't seem too excited about the show.

As I listened to them discuss "more natural" ways to meet a significant other, I became absorbed in how much care she put into whisking the pancake batter before pouring it onto the griddle. She teased the pan this way and that until the pancake took on the shape of a heart. She prepared a plate with the fluffy goodness and then poured vibrant red syrup over the top, spelling out my name inside the heart. Impressive.

Once we'd gone back out front and had taken a seat, I turned to Jacob. "Can I ask you a question?"

He sipped his coffee. "Sure."

"Do you seek out people who hate the idea of the show?" I asked.

"Just trying to keep it real," he said.

"Trying very hard, I've noticed," I said digging into my pancake and closing my eyes in sheer joy as I tasted the light as a feather dessert. "You're lucky you brought me to good food."

His mouth curved upward. "Am I?"

"Filming a television show is exciting. Most people, chosen randomly on a street, would agree. But you..."

"I don't watch much TV. Sorry."

"It seems like there's more to it," I said, since he was going out of his way to introduce me to people who don't like the idea.

He shrugged, taking another sip of coffee.

"That's your story and you're sticking to it," I said, rolling my eyes and giving up. "So, Jacob, if you don't watch TV then what *do* you like to do with your spare time?"

"I have various projects that keep me busy," he said, looking so relaxed and at home in this café that I couldn't help but imagine him as one of the contestants. He certainly looked like a star with those blue eyes and tousled blond hair. "I read a lot. It helps me unwind."

"What kind of books?" I asked.

"I'm currently reading an old favorite, actually. *To Kill a Mockingbird*."

My chest burst with surprise. "I love that book."

He quoted the book and I finished the quote for him. We both smiled.

As we enjoyed our pancakes and hot drinks, we continued talking about the book and other books we liked until I lost track of time. By the end of the meal, my cheeks hurt from laughing so much. When Lauren finally set down the check, Jacob and I reached for it at the same time. His hand grazed mine, sending tingles along my skin. I withdrew my shaky hand.

Since he'd beat me to the bill, I made him promise to let me get the next one. I also realized that the end of the tour had felt more like the end of a date. A *good* date. After chatting with Jacob one-on-one, I now wanted to learn even more about him.

CHAPTER FIVE

After the warmth of Prancer's Pancake House, stepping out into the cold sent chills up and down my spine. Or maybe that was from standing so close to Jacob. Either way, I went to fasten my coat and messed something up because the zipper became stuck. Oh, no. I fumbled with it, but my hands were cold and it wouldn't loosen.

"Want some help?" Jacob asked.

My cheeks heated. "And here I thought I was being discreet."

"Happens to all of us," he said, stepping toward me. He took hold of my zipper, teased the fabric away from the metal teeth and then slowly pulled it up to my chin, his eyes never leaving mine. My heart raced. Crazy thoughts ran through my mind like what it would be like to kiss him. At the same time that I was imagining how it would feel to press my lips to his, another part of my brain realized Jacob was saying something to me.

I blinked. "I'm sorry. What?"

"I asked what you'd like to do now..."

I didn't think "kiss you" would be an appropriate answer,

but I was surprised he wasn't ready to end his day of work. "You're up for continuing the tour?"

"Unless you have someplace else to be."

"No, not at all," I said, stifling a yawn. My body ached to sleep, but I rationalized that continuing the tour would be good for my report. "Can we see the skating rink?"

"Absolutely," he said, turning to me with a serious expression. "With all of the padding they have for skating nowadays, it will dull the pain if you knock me over again."

I laughed. "Ha-ha. Very funny. Besides, I only need to *see* the rink, not skate there."

"I'm afraid you might be disappointed," he said, his arm brushing mine as we walked down the sidewalk. "It's nothing like the one you have at Rockefeller Center."

My gaze whipped to his. "You've been to New York?"

"Nope," he said.

I stopped walking and thrust my hand to my heart. "Do you mean to tell me you saw the skating rink in front of Rockefeller Center on a *television?*?"

"Technically, I saw it on the big screen at a drive-in movie theatre."

"That counts, Jacob. You're not getting off on a technicality."

"Already did," he said, looking proud of his logic. "I watched my favorite movie on this *screen*, which, by the way, is not to be confused with a TV."

I rolled my eyes. "So, what's your favorite movie?"

"Guess."

"Hmm." I wracked my brain for a movie that featured a skating rink. "*Home Alone 2?*"

He shook his head. "*Elf.*"

I burst into laughter. "Will Farrell's *Elf?*"

He nodded. "Best Christmas movie *ever.*"

"I can't disagree with you on that," I said, surprised we liked the same movie. As we continued walking, we chatted about Christmas movies and the inevitable debate came up about whether *Die Hard* counted as one or not. After much discussion, we decided that a Christmas movie should contain elves, sleighs, and of course, Santa Claus himself.

"Okay, here we are," Jacob said.

I looked at the rink, my mouth stretching into a smile. "You're right, it's not the rink at Rockefeller Center. It's better."

Snowflake Skating Rink may be only a fraction of the size of the rink in New York, but it was adorable and magical. Fairy lights lit up the rink and were reflected on the ice. Next to the seating area stood a couple of miniature log cabins which served, judging by the smell, mulled wine, cocoa, and . . . what was that other scent? Of course, cinnamon! I guessed there probably were freshly made tasty treats, also.

"Have you skated here before?"

"Since I was a kid," he said.

"It's beautiful," I said, glancing up at the mountain which towered over this darling town protectively. Lights dotted between the trees as the sun began to fade.

"How about it, Lacey?"

"How about what?" I asked, turning back to Jacob.

He nodded toward the rink. "I will if you will . . ."

"Only if we race," I joked, suddenly feeling the urge to skate.

"You might live to regret that offer," he said, his eyes twinkling as he put a hand on the small of my back. We walked toward the counter for rentals, but Jacob continued past it.

"Where are you going?" I asked.

"I'm your guide, remember?" He gave me a side-glance, the corner of his mouth lifting. "This is part of the tour in case your television star sweethearts skate here."

"Yes, but the rental counter is back there," I pointed out.

He gestured at the counter. "That's not good enough for your soon-to-be famous couples."

"It's not?" I asked, wondering what he had up his sleeve.

"We're going to the master for our skates. Come on, this way."

Beyond the rental counter sat a wooden building. I could hear the sounds of tapping and scraping coming from within the walls. Jacob parted the beaded curtain covering the open doorway, and tiny Santas and snowmen jangled merrily against each other as they were dropped into place behind us.

"Mr. Clauson?" Jacob called, rather loudly. But when Mr. Clauson appeared from behind the work bench, I could see why. He looked to be a hundred years old. Jacob greeted him loudly and slowly, and the old man tilted his head as if attempting to hear better.

"Mr. Clauson, I'd like you to meet Lacey Lane. She's visiting from New York to check out Christmas Mountain for a TV show she produces. I'm showing her the real town, and there's no-one more Christmas Mountain than you. Am I right?"

Mr. Clauson smiled a toothy grin. "That's right."

"Nice to meet you," I said, giving a little wave. "You've lived here a long time?"

"I've been here almost as long as the mountain behind us." He laughed heartily, which turned into a cough. "Excuse me. Now, what can I do for you?"

"We're looking around, getting a feel for the place."

Mr. Clauson scrunched his face. "A chemical peel for the

face? I've read about those in Mrs. Clauson's magazines and they sound horrific."

My eyes widened as he turned to me.

"Why would a pretty young lady like yourself want to go messing with her face? Spend some time in Christmas Mountain and your skin will be glowing better than that peel nonsense. I can promise you that."

"Thanks for the advice," I said, struggling to contain the laughter bubbling up in my chest at Mr. Clauson's outburst. I didn't dare look at Jacob because out of the corner of my eye I noticed his shoulders shaking, too.

"No, she's come to have a look around," Jacob said, increasing his volume. "She's a producer on a TV show and they're thinking of filming a season here."

The old man looked relieved. "Ah, TV. Now there's something useful."

"Ha!" I turned to Jacob, smiling profusely.

The corner of Jacob's mouth hitched up and gave me a second look.

"Are you going to take a turn on the ice?" Mr. Clauson asked.

"We would love to." I nodded. I loved this old man already. What a character; we had to have him in the show!

"Well then you'll need a pair of skates. Here, let me get you your own pair."

I turned to Jacob. "The rentals?"

"Special rentals," Jacob said, keeping his volume up. "Mr. Clauson makes beautiful skates, all by hand. Every pair on loan out there . . ." He nodded toward the skate stall outside. "Well, they have all been handmade right here."

Mr. Clauson nodded. "That's right, been doing it since I was knee high to a grasshopper. Now, what size are you, dear?"

He stooped to measure my foot, but the dim lighting and his ancient eyesight made it a bit of a struggle. Jacob gently took the tape measure from his hands.

"Why don't you go and take a break, and I'll do this for you? You know that I know what I'm doing, because I had the best teacher."

Mr. Clauson shuffled toward the door. "That you did, Jacob. That you did."

When the shed was empty, Jacob got down on one knee, took my foot in his hand, and eased it out of the snow boot. He rested my foot against his denim-clad thigh and started taking measurements, writing down a series of numbers on his hand.

Since I was still standing, I lost my balance a little and instinctively put my hand on his head to steady myself. My fingers felt his soft, blond hair before I pulled away. I wobbled again and he put both hands on my hips to steady me.

He looked up at me. "You promised not to knock me over, remember?"

My mouth spread into a slow smile. "I *never* promised."

He grinned and then stood, taking the measurements to Mr. Clauson. A few moments later he returned, holding out a beautiful white leather boot. As he knelt and slipped my foot into the boot, my imagination ran wild. Suddenly (in my head, of course), I morphed into a snow princess as my snow prince fitted me with my own magical skates.

My heartrate kicked up and I shook my head to clear the thought. This place certainly knew how to weave a spell on me. Hopefully it would do that for the stars on the show, as well.

Jacob sat down on a wooden bench and laced up a pair

of well-worn skates. "I've had these for years. This is the first pair I made under Mr. Clauson's watchful eye.'

I eyed them suspiciously. "They look well-used. You skate often?"

"On occasion." He shrugged, and we traipsed out to the rink, then slipped off the blade guards and stepped onto the ice. A few people glided gracefully around, and I slipped my coat off, knowing that between panic and exertion I would soon build up a sweat.

"You go and skate, while I just, um, find my ice-feet," I said.

"Okay," he said, skating elegantly away. He did a couple of laps in the time it took me to take only a few steps. But as he glided to a stop in front of me, showering me with ice, I let go of the side and slowly slid away from the edge.

Jacob looked amused. "You have skated before, right?"

I put my hands on my hips. "Yes. . . I'm just a bit rusty, that's alllllllll!" The last word came out as a squeal as my arms flailed around like a windmill as I fought to catch my balance. Jacob reached out and steadied me, and my belly did a little flip.

"Thanks," I said, feeling the weight of his arm around me. "It may have been longer than I realized since I've been on the ice."

"Quite a bit longer," he teased.

I went to swat him playfully but wobbled again.

Jacob grabbed my hand to steady me. "Are you ready?"

"I think I can balance now," I said, my heart hammering in my chest.

"Okay." He let go of my hand and began gliding backwards, encouraging me to skate toward him. I was doing okay until a teenager flew past me, startling me, and I flailed once again, reaching out my hand for Jacob to save me. He reached for my hand and this time he didn't let go.

As we skated along, I wondered if he liked holding my hand or if he just didn't want me to fall on my face. Probably the latter. In the end, I didn't do too badly and only fell three times, almost pulling Jacob down with me each and every time. But when my ankles started aching, I knew it was time to call it a day. Jacob kept hold of my hand until we reached the side.

"There you go, safe and sound," he said.

"Thanks," I said, lifting my lashes to find him peering down at me from inches away. The wind blew a strand of my hair across my cheek and I could see my breath come out in a little white puff of air that dissipated.

His gaze held mine as he tucked the strand behind my ear, his fingers grazing my cheek and causing little butterflies to take up residence in my belly. Was he going to kiss me? I held my breath and leaned forward ever so slightly—

"Jacob! How *are* you?" a female voice asked.

I moved back, stumbling off balance yet again. I turned to see a beautiful blonde hurrying over to where Jacob stood, a couple feet away from me now.

"Hi... How are you?" he asked.

"Better now that I've seen your handsome face," she said, continuing up to him and pulling him into a tight embrace. She kissed him on both of his cheeks. "It's so good to see you. Isn't it good to see me?"

He laughed. "Of course."

Without even glancing my way, she leaned in again and kissed his cheek a second time. "You have my number. *Use* it," she said, walking away and glancing coyly back at him.

A weird feeling came over me. Was Jacob dating this woman? Was he dating a lot of women? Not that it was any of my business. I sat down on a bench, feeling irritated as I tugged at my boots, which Mr. Clauson had gifted me.

Jacob sat on the bench opposite to mine and began unlacing his boots.

"Why didn't you introduce me to your friend?" I asked, trying to keep the irritation out of my voice. "She'd look great on camera."

Yeah, over my dead body.

Jacob looked sheepish. "Would it be awful if I said I couldn't remember her name?"

"You . . ." My voice trailed off as I realized he couldn't be dating her then. Relief flooded through me, which made no sense since I'd only spent one day with this guy and half of it had been pretty unpleasant.

He shook his head. "Embarrassing, huh?"

"Comic relief for a scene." I smiled, secretly delighted, and reminding myself that I had no business being jealous. I had two weeks in Christmas Mountain for work, not a winter romance. But the second thought was starting to sound equally appealing to me.

CHAPTER SIX

We walked back to the Sugar Plum Inn in a comfortable silence. I took in all the festive scenes around me with darkness settling and colorful lights dotting the buildings. My first day in Christmas Mountain had been magical and now more than ever I wanted to film season four here. I couldn't wait to report my findings to Mel. When I glanced at Jacob he was smiling.

"What?" I asked.

He shrugged. "I enjoy watching your reaction to Christmas Mountain. There's a reason most of us who are born here, stay here, and those who do leave always find their way back eventually. It's a special place to live."

I nodded. "Christmas Mountain does have a magical air to it."

He nudged me playfully. "Are you falling under the spell, Lacey?"

I swallowed. "You mean of the town, right?"

His eyebrows rose. "What else would I mean?"

"Just checking," I said, letting out the breath I'd been holding. "I was just thinking about the incredible pancakes at Prancer's Pancake House. I mean, who wouldn't fall in love with those?"

His eyes twinkled. "They are pretty special, aren't they? What Lauren can't do with a griddle isn't worth knowing."

I skipped ahead of him and then turned to face him, walking backwards. "I know, right? The way she handled that heart was nothing short of spectacular." I yelped as my foot slipped off the curb. As I fell backward with my arms flailing, I imagined landing like a misshapen snow angel in the street. Instead, firm arms caught me.

Jacob's blue eyes were steady. "You okay?"

"That'll teach me to get excited," I said, my face heating. I wasn't sure if that was because I had just slipped clumsily or because Jacob was still holding my arms, even though I had both feet firmly planted on the ground again. "Yes, I'm fine. Thanks to you."

The corner of his mouth lifted. "If there had been a pot of cacti behind you then I might've reconsidered."

"They were poinsettias," I said, savoring being in his arms.

"If you say so," he said, releasing me as we started to walk again.

I was dying to ask him about the woman at the skating rink, but I wasn't sure how to tackle it without sounding like I was prying. Or interested. Both of which, of course, were true.

"So, was the lady from the skating rink born and bred in Christmas Mountain?" I blurted. So much for minding my own business.

"Who?"

"The totally drop-dead gorgeous woman?" I prodded.

His eyebrows came together and he gave me a side-glance.

I let out a short breath. "The woman who wants you to *call* her?"

He ducked his head a little. "Oh, right."

"Right," I said, wondering how that aggressive woman had slipped from his mind.

"No, she's not a local. She comes here every winter for a vacation," he said, nodding toward the slopes. "Her family has a lodge up the mountain."

"And?" I prompted.

His forehead crinkled. "And what?"

I nudged him playfully. "Is there something between you two? I'm asking purely for research purposes, of course."

He gave me a look I couldn't read and then finally shook his head. "No."

My mouth fell open. "Why not? She's *so* into you."

"Come on, Lacey." Jacob thrust his hands deep into his jacket pockets. He wasn't wearing gloves and his hands must have been freezing. I assumed he didn't normally just stroll along Main Street while showing TV producers around, so his long legs would usually get him home before the cold had a chance to set in.

I picked up my pace a little. "She's beautiful."

He fell into step next to me. "Not my type."

My heart soared, but I kept my expression blank. "She looks like every man's type."

"You think I'm that shallow?"

I bit my lip. "I guess she wouldn't be your type if you're already seeing someone..."

"Let me show you something." He motioned to a wooden bench at the side of the road. "Do you see this dedication?"

I sat down, ran my hand across a brass plaque on the back and read the engraved letters, "In loving memory of

Chuck and Nora, who spent their whole lives loving each other and Christmas Mountain."

He sat next to me and rested his elbows on his knees. "Chuck and Nora were one of Christmas Mountain's biggest love stories. They were born in the same hospital just one day apart and lived next door to each other as kids. They were inseparable. From the day they got married, they never spent a night apart."

"Wow. And . . . what happened?"

His blue eyes peered over at me. "After seventy-five years of marriage, they died within one day of each other."

My eyes filled up. "Oh, that's tragic."

He shook his head. "What would have been tragic is if one of them had settled for a pretty face without a connection. Instead, they lived their lives with their soulmate until it was time to move on. It's like they couldn't survive without the other." He was silent for a moment. "That's my type."

My eyes widened. "But a love like that is rare, isn't it?"

"Rare only makes it more special," he said, his fingers forming a steeple. "Too many people date because they don't want to be alone. I get that, I really do, but the problem is *settling* for one relationship would mean missing out on the real thing."

I thought about my own background. "I still think a love like that is rare, though. I mean, do you know any other love stories like Chuck and Nora? Honestly?"

He nodded and smiled. "Yep. My mom and dad."

I sat back on the bench, intrigued. Despite the cold, these stories of true love were warming my heart better than any heating blanket. "Tell me about them."

He sat up and leaned back in the bench. His shoulder brushed against mine, sending a shiver up my arm. "My parents met at a local production of The Nutcracker. It was a required school field trip and my dad was there under duress since he thought the ballet was just for girls."

"That's ridiculous."

"Nevertheless, he was not too happy to be there," Jacob said, chuckling. "But he told me that when he saw Mom sitting a couple rows in front of him, it was love at first sight. He swapped places with her best friend so he was sitting next to her for the rest of the show. By the time they came out it was the beginning of a great love."

I put a hand to my chest. "That's so romantic."

"Their first official date was to The Nutcracker ballet, of course. Mom's favorite scene was the Dance of the Sugar Plum Fairy. Since then, Dad's nickname for my mom is his "sugar plum fairy." When they decided to open the inn together, Dad named it The Sugar Plum Inn in honor of Mom."

I let out a wistful sigh. "So, the name of their business reminds them of their love every single day. That is definitely a love worth waiting for."

Emotion swirled in Jacob's eyes. "Dad says every time Mom answers the phone and says the name of the inn, they look at each other and think about how they met."

My eyes watered. "That's a beautiful story."

He nodded. "My parents are my role models. Anything less than what they have would never be enough for me."

We were both silent for a moment or two.

"Have you ever been in love, Jacob?" I asked, stealing a glance at him.

He looked into the distance. "Once, maybe. I thought it was love, but . . . it didn't last." He turned to me. "What about you?"

It was my turn to stare into the distance. "I've dated, here and there. But . . ."

"But?"

I couldn't quite meet his gaze. "I guess I've . . . learned not to need anyone too much. My ex called me a workaholic."

"Is that what you are?" he asked.

"I suppose," I said, shrugging. "I actually grew up . . . in the foster care system. Needless to say, that made me become very self-sufficient. Work is the one thing that makes me feel secure. I've moved so much in my life that I'm saving for my own apartment. If this project gets approved then I'll have enough for my down payment."

I closed my eyes, unable to believe all that I'd just revealed. What was wrong with me? Growing up in foster care was something I didn't even like to think about let alone talk about or share with a virtual stranger. I braced myself for whatever Jacob might say or think of me now.

He touched my gloved hand. "May I ask what happened to your parents? If you don't want to tell me, I'll understand."

Somehow, I believed him. My heart pounded in my chest as I worked up the nerve to answer.

"I never knew my birth father, if you want to call him that," I said, the word "father" feeling foreign on my tongue. "I lived with my mom until I was about seven. She had a drug problem and a theft problem related to getting money for drugs. Not exactly stable. After being pulled away from my mom many times for neglect, I finally got put into the system."

"I'm sorry, Lacey."

I glanced at him, trying to gauge if he thought less of me. But there was no judgment in his blue eyes, only kindness. I let out a long breath. "One of the reasons I love my job is that every time our couples find love it gives me hope that happily-ever-after does exist . . . that it's at least possible," I said, a shiver rolling through me.

"A valid point." He stood, offering his hand to help me up. I put my hand in his and he squeezed as I got to my feet. He kept hold of my hand for a few seconds as we started walking but then he let go and slipped his hands into his jacket pockets.

It was only a short walk back to the inn, and I was grateful for the warmth from the fire as Jacob pushed open the door and stood back to let me pass.

"Ruby?" Jacob called as he shrugged his coat off and hung it on one of the hooks by the door. He took my jacket and hung it next to his, which felt so natural it surprised me. "You back?"

A strange noise reached us both at the same time, and Jacob followed the sound with a grin on his face. He walked to the couch in front of the fire and beckoned me over quietly. Ruby was sprawled out on the couch, her mouth wide open as she snored.

"Is that . . . ?"

He nodded. "Yep. Duct tape in her hair."

As Jacob tried to remove the piece of tape gently from her hair, she snored again and called out "Ribbons!" as she slept.

Posters of the lost dog were strewn on the floor where they must have fallen off her lap, and the offending duct tape roll was still gripped in Ruby's right hand.

Jacob slid one arm under his sister's knees and the other under her shoulders and whispered to me, "Could you just pick those posters up for me while I put Ruby to bed in the office?"

He headed for the stairs and I watched his retreating back, wishing I had a brother to take care of me so sweetly.

To tell the truth, it made me realize how alone I really was. It would be wonderful to have Jacob—correction, someone *like* Jacob—in my life.

It was then that I realized Jacob hadn't answered my question about whether or not he had anyone in his life right now. I couldn't help feeling a little bummed at that thought.

CHAPTER SEVEN

After jotting down notes on today's outing until my eyes could stay open no longer, I crawled into bed. My head hit the pillow and I sighed with relief as I waited for blissful sleep to come. I'd been up for forty hours and it was a wonder I hadn't passed out by now.

My head became foggy. Sleep seemed so close and then blue eyes appeared in my mind, making my belly flutter. Jacob was different than any guy I'd ever met. His half-smile threatened to undo me. His stories about true love inspired me. I wondered how I could work those stories into the TV show. Tomorrow. There would be time for these thoughts tomorrow...

PING!

Did I just imagine that noise?

PING!

Was that my phone?

PING! PING! PING!

My eyes flew open. The screen on my cell lit up from its spot on my nightstand. Yep, my phone. I groaned and reached for it, seeing that I had yet another text message from Mel.

Lacey, how's the hunt for locations going?

Lacey, have you found the right pacing for the opening credits yet?

Lacey, can you send me photos or footage of the town so I can work on some of the scenes?

After reading several more of these, I switched my phone to silent and turned on my side. I kept my back to the night stand so I wouldn't be disturbed every time the screen lit up if he sent more messages. But after about ten minutes of squeezing my eyes shut and trying to force sleep to come, I turned over in bed to get comfier only to be met with my screen lighting up for the hundredth time.

I need those shots ASAP.

Uh-oh, he'd dropped the 'Lacey' at the beginning of the text, which meant he was getting irate. Mel had a typical showbiz temperament and if he wasn't getting his way then he'd throw one of those hissy fits he was well known for in New York.

My fingers flew across the screen as I shot him back a text: *Mel, hi, it's been a long day and I'm exhausted. I'll send you the shots in the morning, okay?*

PING!

Long day? You don't know the meaning of the word long! I've been in this office since six a.m. and I'm not finished yet. I NEED those shots.

It appeared that Mel had (conveniently) forgotten that I had left for the airport at four o'clock this morning after zero sleep. Clearly, I could give him a run for his money in a 'who's had the longer day' contest.

I sighed, irritated, and threw back the blankets on the bed. Sleep was not going to happen right now, so I may as well give Mel what he wanted. I swung my legs out of bed and sat up, rubbing my eyes to get the sleepiness out of them.

My throat felt dry, so I needed a drink and remembered that Ruby had told me that I was welcome to use the kitchen at any time. So, I threw on a red sweater over my pajama top, and wondered if I should put on a pair of pants, but decided that the pajama shorts would do. I had a feeling that Christmas Mountain peeps were early to bed and early to rise, so I doubted I'd bump into anyone. I slipped on a pair of fluffy purple socks and headed to the door.

As I opened it, I heard a strange noise coming from upstairs. Peeking over the bannister, I looked downstairs and saw that the lights and the fire were out, although the residual heat from the fireplace still warmed me as it climbed its way up. I stood and listened for a moment and there it was again—the rhythmic sound of . . . *something*. Huh. I wasn't sure what could be causing that sound. Curiosity got the better of me and I decided to forego hot chocolate in favor of being nosy. So, I climbed the narrow stairs which led to what I assumed was the attic.

Maybe one of the family was looking for something in that dusty rarely used space? Like more Christmas ornaments or wood for the fire? I pictured cobwebs and old boxes, but when I reached the top of the stairs, I looked through the doorway into what was probably the coziest apartment of the inn!

The walls of the attic were pine, and there were work benches placed throughout the open space with doors leading off to other rooms. Piles of wood were stacked in corners of this room and some longer pieces were leaning against the walls. Various tools sat on tables and in boxes. On each work bench were what appeared to be toys in various stages of assembly: a toy soldier here, a wooden drum there, and all the traditional toys you would expect to find in an old fairytale.

But what made the room so cozy was the little den at the far end of the room. A winged armchair sat in front of a wood burner, which was casting a warm glow across the room. A soft cream rug sat on the floor in front of the chair. A smaller version of the downstairs Christmas tree stood in one corner, and fairy lights twinkled and sparkled as they flickered on and off. A small bookshelf stood to the side of the chair, with books stacked on it, although I couldn't see any of the titles. It was like Santa's own workshop!

My eyes widened, though, when I realized I wasn't alone. I spotted Jacob's back as he sat at one of the workbenches, facing away from me and rhythmically sanding something that was out of my sight.

I swayed from one foot to the other, torn between making my presence known and continuing to watch Jacob, who was now running his hand along the smooth wood. He had obviously showered after he'd put Ruby to bed because his hair was still damp and he was wearing a different t-shirt than he'd worn under his jacket today. I couldn't help but think that he might need yet another shower before he went to bed because tiny wood shavings danced in the air before settling into his hair.

Intrigued by what he was doing, I took a step forward in order to see better. As I lifted my foot it connected with a small scrap of wood and accidentally kicked it across the room.

Thwack!

Jacob's eyes flicked to where the piece of wood hit the wall and his gaze shot to me.

I wiggled my fingers. "Um, hi."

"Lacey." His face registered surprise and his brow crinkled. "Is everything okay?"

"Just groovy." My shoulders tightened as it occurred to me that he might be annoyed with me invading his private space. Oops. "Well, you know, besides a little clumsiness."

His mouth curved into a smile. "Thought you'd be sacked out by now," he said.

"This is one of those unfortunate situations where I'm so tired I *can't* sleep," I said, feeling embarrassed that I'd been caught spying on him. I turned to leave. "Sorry to bother y—"

"Come in." He stood and waved me over to the bench where he'd been working.

"You sure?" I asked, not wanting to intrude.

"Of course," he said, motioning for me to come in further.

I gave him an appreciative smile and came closer to see what he'd been making. A long piece of wood lay on the table with one end curved elegantly upwards, while another identical piece leaned against the wall next to the bench. Several slats of wood were piled next to it.

"What are you making?" I asked.

"It's a sled." Jacob picked up the piece of wood that was leaning against the wall and placed it next to the one on the bench. Then he picked up some of the slats and laid them side by side between the two curved pieces. "See? This will be the seat, and these two longer pieces of wood are the runners. I'm making it to sell at the Silver Bells Luxury Tours store."

"Is that the shop with the gold letters on the front window?" I asked, watching him nod. I moved closer and stood next to him. "It's beautiful, Jacob. I didn't know you made things out of wood. You're very clever."

He smiled. "Thanks. When I have a beautiful piece of wood, the item almost makes itself."

"But, isn't all wood the same?"

"No, not at all. Let me show you." He picked up the runner he'd been sanding, came up beside me and set it down. Then he took my hand, placed it against the wood and glided my fingertips across the smooth surface. "This is maple."

My belly did a little flip. Oh, *wow*. I so wanted him to do that again.

"See how smooth the wood feels to touch?" he asked, his mouth next to my ear.

"Uh-huh," I said, barely able to form those syllables.

He kept moving my hand along the surface until my arm was stretched out and his body pressed against my side so as to maintain contact with my hand. I could barely breathe, and it wasn't because of the heady smell of wood and sawdust in the room. Lacing his fingers through mine, he began to pull my hand back in the opposite direction.

Then he let go of my hand and picked up another piece of wood, and set it on the table next to the maple. Again, he took my hand and placed it on the wood.

"This is oak. I haven't sanded this one, but see how it feels slightly different? Those little nuances of textures are from the knots." Our hands hovered over a darker mark in the wood, and circled over it, the knot slightly rougher to the touch as it ticked my palm. "These knots are flaws in the wood, but they're natural flaws so they only add to the beauty. Don't you think?"

I swallowed hard, and nodded. "F-flaws can be good."

Jacob held my hand a moment longer and then he slowly untangled his fingers from mine, setting the oak wood back in its place.

I felt slightly faint, sucked in a deep breath, and promptly coughed as I inhaled a lungful of sawdust. How embarrassing. I kept coughing into my elbow as Jacob handed me a bottle of water. I drank deeply from it, conscious that his lips had likely been around the top before mine. The thought may have made me sway a little.

"Thank you," I said, clearing my throat. "Do you make these for a living? In addition to working at the inn?" I asked, looking around at all the different pieces he'd made. It seemed like an eclectic mix of items.

He shook his head. "No, I do this to relax. This is my downtime. Some people watch TV... I make stuff."

I gave him a look to see if he was making a joke but he seemed serious. My mouth pursed as I considered what he was saying.

He shrugged. "This is my escape, my man cave, if you like. I come here to de-stress, or to take time out."

I laughed, mostly to break myself out of the spell he'd cast on me. "Many men go to the gym to de-stress."

To my relief, he laughed, too. "I go for runs and work out with weights. Plus, I get plenty of exercise helping out around the inn. You'd be surprised how much exercise chopping wood is."

I looked at his biceps under the straining fabric of his shirt and nodded.

"Making things takes time and it's slow. But bringing out the beauty in wood and turning it into something that will be cherished and enjoyed, well, that's worth every minute."

"Sounds like a good hobby," I said, wandering around the attic, more to put a physical distance between us than anything. If I stood too close then I might give in to the strong urge I had to kiss him.

I ran my hand along the top of a table, which had the

beginnings of a heart carved into it. "What's the most special item you've made? There must be one thing that will always stay with you."

He nodded without hesitation. "There is."

I looked around the room. In all honesty, it was hard to pick just one beautiful object out of so many. There were tables and chairs, a headboard, and even a rocking chair with elaborate carvings in the back.

"So, what is it? Will you show me?"

"You've already seen it."

My eyebrows came together. "I have?"

He smiled. "Yep, you sat on it."

My eyes widened. "Chuck and Nora's bench! You made that?"

"Yep. It was going to be a seventy-sixth wedding anniversary gift for them, to go in their yard, but . . ."

My eyes watered. "But they died before you could give it to them?"

He nodded. "We decided to put it on Main Street so people could rest and remember them."

I was touched. "That's beautiful, Jacob."

He pressed his lips together, but didn't say anything.

"Hey Jacob," I said, biting my bottom lip. "You didn't answer my question earlier."

He looked quizzically at me. "What question was that?"

My gaze held his and my throat went dry. "Is there anyone special in your life?"

"Is this research for your show?" he asked.

I swallowed. "Of course."

"In that case . . ." He took a step toward me, tucking a wisp of hair behind my ear as all of the air went out of my lungs. "You should know . . . I don't do TV interviews."

"Oh," I said, as his finger skimmed the sensitive spot behind my ear, sending shivers along my skin. Gulp.

"But, I'm single," he said, his blue eyes seeming to peer right inside me. "If that's what you wanted to know."

A silence fell between us as we stared at each other. Suddenly, I felt way too exposed.

"I should get some sleep," I said, taking a step back. He stayed where he was, letting me retreat toward the door on wobbly legs. "Good night, Jacob," I said.

"Sweet dreams, Lacey," he replied.

With that, I escaped out the door with my heart pounding as I descended the stairs, holding my breath until I was safe in my room with the door closed behind me. It felt like something had just happened between us and I had no idea what that meant. But I did have dreams that night and they all starred Jacob, who tucked my hair behind my ear over and over again followed by a long kiss that melted me to my core.

CHAPTER EIGHT

The next morning, I woke with a smile and snuggled into my pillow, remembering the dream I'd been immersed in moments ago. Jacob and I were standing in front of the fire in the lounge area downstairs and we heard a strange noise. We looked up and saw mistletoe growing and spreading across the ceiling. It did not occur to me for this to be an odd thing. Instead, I felt wonder and excitement at the growing green plant.

Nestled in my dream again, I did think it was a little weird that instead of working at Prancer's Pancake House Lauren stood in the room with us, shaking a griddle in the corner making the mistletoe form a heart above our heads. But I smiled as Jacob took my face in his hands and kissed me, slowly and tenderly and *very* fully on the lips.

Eh-Eh-Eh-Eh!

The sudden blaring of my alarm clock made my eyes pop open and I bolted upright in bed. Where was I? This was not my New York apartment bedroom. Okay, wait. Plane ride. Christmas Mountain Sugar Plum Inn. It was all becoming clear now, which is why my conversation with

Jacob last night in his work room must've invaded my brain. I cringed as I recalled asking him if he was single (twice). Why on earth had I done that? That had nothing to do with my job or the reason I was in Christmas Mountain.

Feeling ridiculous for asking such a personal question, I stood in the shower for a long time, letting the hot water run over me and hoping the cinnamon scented shower gel would wash away memories of my humiliating question and that unrealistic dream. Finally, success. As I turned off the water, the phantom memory of Jacob's lips on mine rolled through my mind. Shiver.

"Nope, still unfocused," I said, wiping the steam from the mirror and staring at my reflection. I started blow-drying my hair, and gave myself a narrowed stare in the mirror.

"Lacey, you know this interest in Jacob is crazy, right?" I asked, as my reflection stared back at me with a blank expression. "You're here for work and a very crucial bonus. Dating might have been acceptable except that 1) Jacob lives in Montana; 2) You live in New York; and 3) You're only here for two weeks. So, stop acting like a lovestruck twenty-eight-year-old, focus on your job, and stop thinking about Jacob Curtis."

I sighed, knowing it was going to be very difficult to forget about him while we were practically living under the same roof. I ran the brush through my now-dry locks and nodded resolutely to myself in the mirror. Time to focus on the reason I came here.

As I tiptoed down the stairs, I could hear Ruby and Jacob talking in the office, and his voice caused my belly to flutter. Not good, Lacey. Not good. I hurried from the stairs to the front door and slipped out before either of them could see me. Checking out potential shoot locations on my own would be safer, so I could leave the mistletoe memories to the contestants.

The walk to Main Street felt strange without Jacob. After spending most of the day together, our banter had become easy and comfortable. Add the fact that I didn't have a clue where I was going or what I wanted to see, the day was already turning out disappointing and it was only—I checked the time on my cell—a little after nine a.m.

After stopping by Prancer's Pancake House to get a Lauren's Luscious Latte to go, I wandered along the side streets, and looked through the window of a quaint little store called Christmas Curiosities. I sipped my coffee and watched the little red and green train chugging its way around the Christmas tree display, and the unusual wooden ornaments which adorned the branches. A wooden robin caught my eye, its chest scarlet and puffed up against the snow decorating the twig on which it stood.

I pushed open the door and walked inside, half-wanting to see if there was anything here that could be used for the show, and half-wanting to buy the robin for my own apartment back home. The shopkeeper smiled at me from behind the counter, and I smiled back, lifting the little bird and turning over the label to see the price: *J.C. Designs*. I frowned, something playing in the back of my mind as I took the item to the counter to pay.

The young woman took the robin from me and wrapped it in sparkly tissue paper. "You have good taste. All of the wooden ornaments are made right here in Christmas Mountain by one of our residents."

"Which resident, may I ask?"

"His name is Jacob—"

"Curtis?" I finished.

She nodded. "You know him?"

A Sugar Plum Christmas

Not as well as my dreams would like.

"Yes, I'm staying at the Sugar Plum Inn," I said, taking the little bag she held out.

"The family that runs the inn is lovely. Such heart-felt people," she said.

"I've noticed," I said, thinking of Ruby running after someone's lost dog and Jacob carrying his sister to the office to sleep.

"Have a wonderful day," she said.

"Thank you," I said, heading out the door.

Outside, the snow started falling and I thrust my hands deep into my pockets as I headed back to Main Street. In New York, I thrived on striding down the streets by myself. Why was I missing the company of someone I'd just met?

As I passed the bookstore called Rudolph's Reads, I remembered the conversation Jacob and I'd had about books. I smiled, reminiscing about how we'd quoted lines from our favorite book and how we'd finished each other's sentences as we'd discussed the storyline.

My friend Carol had returned to Christmas Mountain last year and had bought this bookstore, which had been her favorite place as a child. I'd been so busy with work I didn't have time to let her know I was coming, but I decided to go in.

A bell tinkled again as I opened the door and Carol's familiar voice floated through from the back of the store, "I'll be there in a minute!"

"No problem," I said, wandering around, running my hands along the spines of the books and breathing in the smell of old volumes. A black-striped tabby cat walked by me swishing his tail.

"As I live and breathe . . . Lacey Lane!" Carol exclaimed,

before running across the room and pulling me into a bear hug. "What are you doing here?"

"It's so good to see you," I said, giving her a squeeze. "Is this your cat?"

"That's Hemi, short for Hemingway. He's the story mascot," she replied.

"How cute," I said, before holding her at arm's length and studying her. She had the same contented glow that a lot of the other Christmas Mountain people seemed to have. This place sure worked its magic on everyone who lived here. "I'm here for work. Scouting the place for a potential season shoot."

"Interesting idea," she said, her eyes wide with excitement.

I was dying to catch up on the gossip (aka: getting the lowdown on Jacob). "How is Tim?"

Her face lit up. "He's great, thanks for asking."

"Glad to hear it," I said, smiling at her and wanting to ask about Jacob but maybe this wasn't the best place. "Do you have time to grab a coffee or brunch? My treat..."

"Sorry, hon, but I have a roomful of women back there and need to mind the store out here, too." She nodded toward a door at the back of the store. "Book club today."

Just at that moment, a shriek of laughter came from behind the door, followed by whoops of delight and then giggles.

"We're not always the quietest bunch," Carol said, grinning. "Hey, why don't you come back and meet everyone? I'd love to introduce you."

I paused. "I don't know..."

"I've told them all about my fabulous friend from New York and they would be so excited to meet you in person," she said, but I still hesitated. "Plus, you know, this would be great research for the show. Getting to know the locals and all, right?"

"Hmm," I said, knowing I couldn't resist a fantastic opportunity for the show. Plus, I loved books. Maybe I would get some good recommendations on top of everything else. "All right. I'm in."

"Good," she said, leading me through the door to the back and into a cozy room filled with armchairs and an open fire.

"Ladies, *this* is my good friend, Lacey Lane. She's the one I've told you about from New York and she's here visiting for ..."

I saw Carol turn to me and I forced a smile. "Just under two weeks."

"Lacey, this is everyone," Carol said, with a nod.

A sea of smiling (and as embarrassed as I was to admit it, star struck) faces greeted me and I gave a self-conscious wave. "Hello everyone."

"Welcome, Lacey! Sit down," a woman said, gesturing to a comfy-looking old armchair.

"Thank you," I said, leaning back into the cozy chair.

"This is exciting. It's not every day we get a celebrity in town," the woman said.

I gave a small smile, since it was hard to get used to people thinking I was a celebrity. Sure, my name was on the credits but the attention usually went to the cast and all of these enthusiastic faces felt a little overwhelming for me.

"Lacey, this is Harmony," Carol said, gesturing to the woman who'd spoken.

The blonde woman in the velvet chair gave a little wave. "That's me."

"Harmony is the manager at Silver Bells Luxury Tours."

Harmony's face lit up as she nodded. "I got promoted

last year when our manager, Faith Sterling, was hired at *It's All Downhill From Here*."

"That's the ski resort you've told me about, right?" I asked, giving Carol a side-glance. She nodded and I turned back to Harmony. "Nice to meet you," I said, smiling at her.

"You, too." Harmony's blue eyes sparkled beneath blonde bangs. She wore the biggest, friendliest smile I'd ever seen and I liked her immediately.

"I love your show. If Carol had told me you were coming to town, I would've done a happy dance." She wiggled her hips in demonstration.

I laughed, finding Harmony's exuberance infectious. "In Carol's defense, it was a last-minute trip so she had no idea."

Carol gestured toward a woman with brown eyes and blonde hair pulled back into a tight bun. "And this is Macy Wilcox. Macy makes the most delicious cookies in town. Her business, Macy's Morsels, delivers service to all the best stores and businesses here and in nearby towns."

"Nice to meet you," Macy said, her deep dimples appearing as she looked shyly at me, clearly much more introverted than the extroverted Harmony.

"I'm surprised to hear of a business without a Christmas connotation in its name," I said, taking a mental note.

Everyone laughed, including Macy, who shrugged. "I do love Christmas, though."

"And this is Giselle," Carol, said turning toward a woman who looked quiet and studious, but behind horn-rimmed glasses her eyes twinkled mischievously. "She's our resident writer, who lives a reclusive life in a tiny wooden lodge on the mountain as she writes the great American novel."

"You make me sound like a hermit, Carol," Giselle said, letting out a boisterous laugh that I recognized from when I was out front earlier. "Seriously, I'm only allowed out for food or if I'm stuck on a particularly grueling scene."

"Basically, that's every day," Harmony joked.

"And not so reclusive," Giselle added, with a chuckle.

"Unless she's on a deadline," Carol said, raising her eyebrows.

"At those times she won't even answer her cellphone," Harmony said, and the group laughed good-naturedly.

"Giselle? Is that French?" I asked.

She shook her head, her mousy brown hair falling loose from its ponytail. "Ha. I wish. Actually, I was named after a distant aunt who was way more exotic than I am. Me? I'm content in my small mountain town with a keyboard and a cup of coffee."

We all laughed, including Giselle. The feeling of friendship in the group was wonderful. I looked at the lady sitting next to me and smiled. She was sitting back in her chair looking totally relaxed and chilled.

"Hi, I'm Amanda," she said, using the calmest, most soothing voice I'd ever heard.

"Amanda is a massage therapist," Carol said, putting a hand on my shoulder. "She has a room at the C.M. Salon where she practices. She's amazing."

"Yes, I put my clients to sleep," she told me, laughing. I could totally see her doing the job, because her voice was already lulling me into a cozy state of mind.

"Sounds heavenly," I said.

"It so is," Carol said, giving me a wide-eyed look. "I highly recommend going there. It's great for getting rid of unwanted tension."

I inwardly wondered if Amanda could help me get rid of my unwanted tension, namely my infatuation with the innkeeper's son.

"This is Nina . . ." Carol gestured to the lean and tall gal, who had beautiful latte skin. "She works at the Christmas Mountain Country Club and also part-time giving ski lessons on the mountain."

Nina wiggled her fingers at me. "Hi, Lacey."

I smiled back. "Nice to meet you, Nina."

"And finally, this is Brooke, who—"

"Is still trying to come up with a name for the book club," Brooke finished, turning to me in a very business-like way. "We've just formed this badly needed book club and we have no name. Oh, the horror! Hi, how are you?"

"Great, thanks," I said, thinking Mel would love her focused personality.

"Brooke is a teacher at the local high school," Carol explained.

"Who is trying to keep the kids sane and focused until Christmas break," Brooke said. "Sorry, rather stressful time for me trying to get all of the tests graded and book reports reviewed. I'm not this scary, normally. We just can't find a good name for the book club and it's driving me bonkers."

I laughed. "A name for the book club?"

All seven women nodded in unison.

"Maybe you could suggest something?" Carol prompted.

I thought for a moment, and then my eyes landed on the cover of the book they were all holding. *Snow Way I'm Letting Him Go – a winter romance.* A lighthearted romance novel. It reminded me of Jacob holding my hand at the rink, and slipping my skate boot on like a modern-day Cinderella. Then I remembered my dream and the heart that had been formed.

"How about The Mistletoe Book Club?" I offered.

The women all looked at each other for confirmation, before one by one they started nodding and smiling.

"Okay, let's put it to the vote," Carol said, raising her hand. "All those in favor of the name?"

Six additional hands shot up in the air, and The Mistletoe Book Club was born.

"You have to join us, Lacey," Macy said, quietly but firmly.

"We should vote on that suggestion." Carol cleared her throat and raised her hand. "All in favor of Lacey joining the club?"

An excited murmur rose and all hands shot up.

"Sorry, ladies," I said, shaking my head. "I love books a lot, but I'm only here for a couple of weeks and then I'll be going back to New York."

Carol shrugged. "That's what video conferencing is for. You can join us remotely after you leave. But in the meantime, we meet every week here. Bring cake and you're in!"

"I guess it's settled," I said, a warm feeling washing over me. I was genuinely touched. It had taken me months to build up my friendship with Carol when we'd met in New York, but here in this small Montana town, I felt like I'd just made six new friends for life.

CHAPTER NINE

Jacob starred in my dreams again, giving me another restless night's sleep. This time we were ice skating under a star-filled sky and the stars were all green and red like Christmas lights. Despite my dreams, Jacob and I hadn't run into each other yesterday—mostly because I'd avoided the inn. Instead, I explored on my own, took a gazillion photos and sent a lengthy update to Mel. My mind was completely focused on work again. Well, at least for my waking hours.

I got dressed in a hurry, determined to sneak out of the inn again without being seen by Jacob. I came down the stairs, hurried to the entry, pulled the front door open . . . and on the other side of the door in front of me stood Jacob.

His cheeks were pink from the cold and he held a pile of freshly chopped wood in his arms, the woodsy scent drifting up my nose. My heart warmed.

"Good morning, Lacey," he said.

"Hi, Jacob," I said, giving a polite nod as he passed by me.

"Where are you off to this morning?" he asked, speaking

over his shoulder as he walked across the room and set the wood in a bin next to the fireplace.

"Just exploring. Getting to know the town," I said, watching him wipe his hands together as he came back over to me.

"Successful day yesterday?" he asked, seeming curious.

I nodded. "I spent quite a bit of time at Rudolph's Reads."

"That's a great place," he said.

"My friend Carol introduced me to her book club, and I ended up staying and chatting with them for the rest of their meeting. They were really nice," I said, getting the words out so fast I was surprised I hadn't stammered. "Then I wandered in and out of the stores for a bit and then when—"

"Is everything okay?" Jacob asked, putting a hand on my forearm and instantly calming me. "You're going a mile a minute?"

"Sorry," I said, my cheeks heating. "My exploring was . . . productive."

"Good." He tucked a wisp of hair behind my ear and then his brow wrinkled "I'd planned to give you another tour yesterday. But you disappeared without a word."

I bit my bottom lip. "When I came downstairs you were in the back talking to Ruby so I didn't want to disturb you . . ."

He frowned. "You would never disturb me."

Never? Gulp. "Well, I didn't want to *interrupt* you."

"I would never find you an interruption," he said, his voice soft. "Have I done something to upset you, Lacey?"

I shook my head. "No, of course not."

"What then?" He blew out a breath and raked a hand through his blond hair. "Not that you have to take another tour with me. I was just . . . surprised you didn't mention you were leaving."

"I'm sure you have more interesting things to do than babysit me," I said, biting my bottom lip.

He gave me the strangest look. "If you would rather tour by yourself that's fine, I'll stop bugging y—"

"No, it's not that at all," I said, shaking my head.

"I thought we had a good time on the tour the other day," he said, slipping his hands into his pockets.

"We did," I said, quickly, stepping toward him. "You've been great."

"What then?" he asked, his blue eyes looked so earnest.

I sighed. "I'm sorry. You're right. We had a good time and I blew it. Honestly, I'm sure a tour from you would've taught me more than I learned on my own."

He was silent for a moment. "Okay, well, let me know if and when you'd like another tour. No pressure."

"When!" I blurted, letting out a chuckle. "I mean, if you're not busy then I'd love a tour."

That was so the truth. Because, um, it would be way better for my research.

"I've got to get the fire going, but I'm free in fifteen minutes," he said. "That work?"

"Sure, I'll grab a coffee and meet you back here?"

"It's a plan," he said, touching my elbow before he went back to the logs he'd set down.

After getting a to-go coffee and a cinnamon roll from Jingle Bells Bakery—oh, yum—I ate my breakfast on my stroll back to the inn. When I returned, Jacob was out front wearing a thick coat and the navy-blue beanie I'd seen him wearing when we first met.

"You ready?" I asked, dropping my garbage into a green metal trash can with a picture of Santa on it.

"Yep," he said, coming up beside me on the sidewalk. "I figured I could take you up to The Sharing Tree. How does that sound?"

"Lead the way," I said, my 'producer side' kicking in when I heard him say the destination. I'd read a few paragraphs about The Sharing Tree in the brochure on my nightstand and had earmarked it as a possible location for filming.

Jacob glanced down at my white snow boots. "Do you have hiking boots with you? It can get slippery up by the tree, and there are stairs to climb to get up by the Falls."

"Truthfully, all I have are these snow boots," I said, leaving out that they were starting to pinch a little.

"Hold on. I'll go see if Ruby has an extra pair lying around."

A couple of minutes later he returned, carrying a pair of sturdy walking boots. "These will work better."

"Thanks . . ." My voice trailed off as I watched him get down on one knee.

"Lift," he said, gently pulling off my boot. He set the hiking boot under my foot and I slipped it in and watched as he tied up the laces.

"I could get used to this special service," I said, feeling pampered just like when he'd helped me get my ice skates on. I was also touched that he remembered my size.

"We aim to please at the Sugar Plum Inn," he said, the corners of his eyes crinkling as he flashed me a smile. He took my furry boots and dropped them just inside the door. "Let's take you to The Sharing Tree."

Any awkwardness we'd had disappeared as we walked down the street, chatting about my visit to the bookstore. We hiked up the stairs beside the Falls in search of this special tree I'd heard so much about and I realized how right he had been about my boots since the sidewalk seemed particularly icy today. Even without the snow boots, I was slipping and sliding all over the place, which gave me an excuse to hold onto the arm he'd offered.

When we reached the top of the stairs, the path leveled out and I noticed the handrail between the path and the Falls, protecting visitors from slipping over the edge—yikes! We came upon an old wooden bench.

"This bench had a name, right?" I asked, remembering I'd read something about it in the brochure at the inn.

He gave me a side-glance. "Kissing Bench."

My belly warmed. "Oh. Well, that's pretty much the perfect name for a dating show, isn't it?"

"I wouldn't know," he said, pausing by the bench. "Not much for TV, remember?"

"How could I forget?" I joked, giving him a little smile. Were we going to sit on Kissing Bench? I didn't dare ask the story behind the name.

"That is The Sharing Tree," Jacob said, gesturing up the path to the most beautiful tree I had ever seen.

Majestic and huge, The Sharing Tree looked like a grand Christmas tree reaching up toward the sky. As the sun shined down, the rays hit the hundreds of ornaments and trinkets which hung from its branches, making them sparkle.

"I'm ... speechless."

He smiled. "This is a Christmas Mountain icon."

"It's so beautiful." I ran my hand along the back of the wooden bench before I sat down, and turned to Jacob. "Did you ..."

"Make the bench?" he asked, reading my mind as he sat down beside me. He shook his head. "No, this was here long before me. This bench goes back generations."

"Tell me the story behind this place," I said, breathing in the clean mountain air, and then letting out a contented sigh.

He gestured toward the tree. "You see all those ornaments?"

I nodded. "Yes."

"Every single one of those was placed there in remembrance of someone. A lot of the time, we put an ornament on to remember someone who's no longer with us. We *share* our thoughts and love with them, hence the name."

"What a wonderful tradition," I said, taking in all of the ornaments, each one so unique.

"I've been doing this for as long as I can remember," he said, pulling a small box from his pocket and opening it. Inside sat a tiny wooden sled, painted and sprinkled with red glitter. He lifted the beautiful ornament toward me. "I made this in memory of my grandfather."

I took the tiny wooden ornament and held it up, looking at the exquisite detail. "This is so special, Jacob."

"My grandfather taught me everything I know about woodworking. This is a replica of the first sled we made together." He eyed the ornament, bringing his head so close to mine that if I turned a couple of inches to the right, I could have kissed him.

Work, Lacey. Focus on work.

"You see the tiny bits of glitter?" he asked.

I nodded. "I see it."

"When I was a kid, Gramp would sprinkle a tiny amount of glitter over every sled he made. He told me it was magic dust to keep whoever was riding that sled safe. Last night, I put that glitter on here as magic dust to keep *him* safe . . . until we meet again."

My throat tightened. "How thoughtful. It's wonderful

that you had him in your life."

He glanced at me. "He was the best."

I waited for him to hang the ornament on the tree, but instead he opened the tiny box again. I peered inside and watched as Jacob pulled out another ornament. When I saw what it was, I clasped my hand over my mouth. "Oh!"

"I made this for you," he said, placing the tiny wooden object on my upturned palm.

My eyes watered as I examined the tiny pair of snow boots painted white complete with faux fur covering the tops as they stood in a pile of snow, which was sprinkled with white iridescent glitter. The ornament was tiny and perfect. I loved it.

"Jacob, it's beautiful. When did you make this?"

He grinned, obviously pleased with my reaction. "Last night. As a kind of peace offering for whatever I had done to upset you."

"You didn't do anything at all," I said, putting a hand on his arm and then turning my attention back to the little boots. "I should've asked you to show me around again. I wanted to, but . . ."

He waited a minute. "But, what?"

I couldn't exactly tell him I'd been thinking about him in a very "under the mistletoe" way, so I turned back to the ornament. "I don't have anyone to hang this ornament in honor of."

His blue eyes filled with emotion. "Is there anyone special back home you're missing?"

I shook my head. "No. Sometimes I feel safer that way," I admitted.

A line formed between his eyebrows. "Don't you have someone you count on?"

"I have a couple of friends, who I meet for the occasional

lunch." I looked up at the tree, and felt all the love coming from its branches. "We have a good time together, but I'm pretty self-sufficient. Seeing how close you are with your sister makes me see what's been missing from my life. But not everyone is as lucky as you are."

We were silent for a moment.

"You okay?" he asked.

"Oh, I'm fine," I said, waving my hand dismissively. I was used to being left out of family holidays. I turned the ornament over and over in my hand, tiny bits of glitter clinging to my gloves. Although I was supposed to hang it on the tree, I almost didn't want to part with it.

"I've got an idea." He got to his feet and held his hand out to pull me up. "Why don't you hang the ornament for the promise of finding that one special person you can love and trust?"

"Like Chuck and Nora," I said, taking his hand and standing. We walked to the tree and it wasn't lost on me that Jacob was still holding my hand. "You first," I said.

"How about together?" he asked.

I nodded. As Jacob hung his sled, I picked a branch and settled my sparkly boots on one of the lower branches, thinking of finding my one true love. My eyes filled. I mean, why shouldn't it be possible for me to find love? The couples on my show did. Well, sometimes.

As if sensing how I was feeling, Jacob slipped his arm around my waist and pulled me into a hug. With my face buried in his chest, I breathed in his woodsy scent and a feeling of warmth slipped over me. We stayed that way for a long time, embracing by The Sharing Tree, with the sound of the ornaments jingling in the breeze and the rushing waterfall behind us.

And there was no place else I would rather be.

CHAPTER TEN

I spent the next few days exploring Christmas Mountain on my own and found many new locations that would be wonderful for shooting. Every day that passed seemed to further solidify my opinion that filming a season of *Fourteen Days Till Forever* here would be amazing for the contestants and viewers. I'd been browsing studio apartments in the city that I'd be able to afford after I received my bonus (aka: down payment) from Mel after the location approval. I'd narrowed my options down to one, a unit that was light and bright and warm and in a good location—place that I could finally call home in the city.

What I hadn't counted on was how much *this* small mountain town would grow on me.

Grabbing a Lauren's Luscious Latte in the mornings was becoming a habit I didn't want to break. But in a little over a week, I'd be heading back to the city for Christmas. Perhaps I'd volunteer at that soup kitchen like I did last year. They already had my donation check and the volunteer slots were filled, but I could always double check since I didn't have any plans.

Quite the opposite of the Sugar Plum Inn where they were planning a feast for their family and the guests. Being at the inn felt like coming home every night. In fact, this entire town had greeted me with open arms. But I was only here for a short-term work gig. I rationalized that I'd get to see everyone—Lauren, Carol, the book club, Mr. and Mrs. Curtis, Ruby, Jacob, and more—again during filming. The thought didn't mollify the ache in my chest.

Since it was Friday night, I told Mel I was switching my phone off for the weekend. This was new for me, but I'd worked hard and deserved a couple days to myself. Not one dinner had gone by without my phone beeping or ringing. Although Mrs. Curtis (Jacob and Ruby's mom) had waved away my apologies, working during a meal suddenly seemed very inappropriate.

The snow was really coming down as I hurried through the inn's front door later than I had planned. I walked in, shrugged off my coat and placed my boots by the fire. I looked around and noticed the dining room was empty. Just then Mrs. Curtis came bustling through from the kitchen and took my coat, shaking the snow off before hanging it on a hook.

"I'm sorry I'm late for dinner, Mrs. Curtis," I said.

"Don't you worry, Lacey. I've kept something warm for you. And please, call me Betty."

She had told me this more than once, but habits were hard to break after being raised in strict foster homes that had taught me to be both respectful and a little scared of adults.

"Thank you . . . Betty," I said, feeling somewhat reassured by the kindness in the blue eyes looking back at me. Blue eyes just like Jacob's.

"Did you have a good day?" she asked.

"Yes, I just lost track of time at a little log cabin outside of town. It was a beautiful location. It will make a wonderful spot to have a scene for the show."

"You work so hard, Lacey. Now it's time to eat." Betty smiled and waved me through to the dining room, gesturing to a table set for two. Then she disappeared into the kitchen and returned, carrying two steaming plates of food. She set one down in front of me and then sat in the opposite chair with the other plate in front of her.

I was aghast. "You didn't wait for me, Mrs. Cu—I mean, Betty, did you?"

She shook her head. "No, dear, I ate a little earlier with the other guests. But you don't get a fine figure like mine by sticking to just one evening meal." She laughed, patting her generous hips. "Besides, everyone is out for the evening, so I thought I'd keep you company. Unless you need to work?"

I patted my pocket where my phone was kept. "Phone is off and I won't be working again until Monday. I'd love the company."

She smiled. "I'm glad to hear it, you work too hard."

"I love my work," I said, diving into the chicken and ham pie in front of me, a cloud of steam escaping as my knife broke through the incredible puff pastry. I was suddenly ravenous and for a few moments we ate in silence while I made appreciative noises, because it really was delicious.

"So how was the rest of your day, Lacey? Apart from the Bear Gulp?"

"Bear Gulp?" I repeated, suddenly a little fearful of being out on my own.

She chuckled. "We call that log cabin Bear Gulp because if you saw a grizzly up there, gulping is the only thing you could do. It's an 'in joke', don't worry. There are not usually bears up there but it keeps the tourists on their toes."

I breathed a sigh of relief. "Phew! I was thinking I'd need a bodyguard when I go out."

She raised an eyebrow. "So, you don't have your own personal bodyguard waiting for you back in New York?"

I laughed. "You mean, a boyfriend? No, there's no one, only me."

She chewed thoughtfully, and then nodded. "Yes, Jacob did mention that you were on your own. He said your mother has been out of your life since you were young?"

I nodded, a stab of sadness slicing my heart.

"I hope you don't mind him telling me, dear. He was just saying what a strong person you are having had to cope alone for most of your life."

"It's amazing how tough you get when you have no other choice," I said, feeling like I didn't do anything special, I just had bad luck in the parent department.

"You'd be surprised how many people just give up when things are hard. But you have persevered. That speaks volumes to your character," she said firmly. Then she dabbed the corner of her misty eyes with a napkin.

"Thank you," I said, appreciating her kindness even though it felt awkward when someone seemed to feel sorry for me—as if I were an outsider or something.

"Lacey, I get the impression that Jacob is . . . well, fond of you," she said, meeting my eye.

"I'm sure he's just being nice," I said, my cheeks going up in flames. But then I remembered the way he'd hugged me by The Sharing Tree. Certainly, that had been more than a friendly gesture.

"Don't be embarrassed, dear. He's quite the catch, you know," she said, with a twinkle in her eye. "His father would tell you that Jacob takes after him, but we both know where he gets his looks and personality from, eh?"

I couldn't help but join in as she laughed heartily. Jacob and Ruby were truly lucky to have a mom like Betty Curtis. The woman oozed humor and kindness.

She wiped both eyes with a corner of her napkin. "I'm not one to give advice, you know. Heaven knows I haven't always gotten things right."

"You seem to have the ideal life," I noted.

"Well then, my advice may be more appealing than I thought. I just think you should open your heart and mind to any possibility. Don't limit yourself."

I tilted my head. "Any possibility?"

"You don't want to rule things out due to distance. That's all I'm saying."

"Actually, I have made some friendships here this week, which is crazy when you think about the distance between Christmas Mountain and New York—"

"Twenty-three hundred miles," she said, as if she'd calculated the drive time.

I stopped chewing and stared at Betty. "That's kind of a specific guess."

She looked back at me with a slight blush coloring her cheeks. "What can I say? We're a family who likes geography."

"I see," I said, wondering if she was trying to play matchmaker with Jacob and me. Did she really want her son to date someone long-distance when there were plenty of women here who would be interested in him? Like the woman at the ice-skating rink, for example. "Well, twenty-three hundred miles is a long way, but luckily there is video conferencing for the book club."

"Oh, yes. Jacob tells me you stumbled upon Carol's book club?" she asked, as if to clarify.

I nodded. "I knew Carol back in New York. In fact, she's the one who told me about Christmas Mountain."

"Very nice," Betty said, finishing off the last of her meal.

"Everyone in the book club was super friendly at the meeting," I said, remembering how I'd felt welcomed right away. In fact, I felt welcome from the moment I stepped inside this inn. "Ruby and Jacob are such warm and friendly hosts to the guests here. You should be proud of both of them."

Her face lit up. "I am, dear, I certainly am."

"What was Jacob like as a child?" I asked, glancing up at her to gauge if I was getting too personal. But if her smile was any indication, she didn't seem to mind my question one bit. "I mean, he's so sweet and patient and caring. Was he always like that?"

"He was a kind soul since the day he was born." She nodded, beaming. "I remember one year when the kids were young, Ruby's best friend's sister died in a tragic accident. Ruby was devastated and Jacob locked himself away in his den upstairs. We thought he was upset about the accident, which he was, of course But when he eventually came out, he gave Ruby a tiny pendant he had made from wood. It was in the shape of a little girl with wings on her back, so that Ruby could keep sweet Grace close to her heart. She still wears it sometimes."

Betty trailed off, deep in thought, and I felt close to tears at Jacob's thoughtfulness. In a world that sometimes seemed full of takers, Jacob was one of life's givers. I felt the sudden urge to do something special for him in return.

And I had *just* the thing in mind.

CHAPTER ELEVEN

After dinner, I excused myself as soon as I'd finished the swoon-worthy apple crumble and custard that followed the pie. I thanked Betty for her hospitality and then slipped upstairs. I wanted to get started on my gift for Jacob and needed a couple of hours alone to do it.

Up in my cozy room, I flipped open my laptop and clicked on a file I'd saved as "Christmas Mountain Outtakes," and grinned as image after image filled the screen. I began putting together a slideshow of the photos I'd taken during my time in Christmas Mountain. These weren't the shots I'd sent to Mel, but these had captured the behind-the-scenes spirit of the town.

As I scrolled through the file, I realized that a great many of the photos were of Jacob. My gaze locked on a photo of the spot where Jacob had fallen into the pot of poinsettias when I had knocked him off his ladder. Next was a photo I had taken of the little wooden robin in the store window, before I'd even found out that Jacob made it.

I'd barely been in Christmas Mountain for a week, but the memories I had amassed were incredible—a shot of my furry snow boots standing next to the fire, a photo of my heart-shaped pancake which Lauren had made for me at Prancer's Pancake House and—oh, *cute!*—there was a picture Lauren had taken with my camera of Jacob and me deep in conversation about books. My heart warmed as I noticed the look on Jacob's face as he listened to whatever I had been saying. I enlarged the shot and zoomed in on his face, a lump forming in my throat at the softness of his gaze as he looked into my eyes with rapt attention.

The next photograph choked me up for different reasons; it was a close up of Chuck and Nora's plaque, with snow clinging to the corners of the brass plate, and the simple words telling the story of a lifetime of love. A little pull tugged at my heart, making me realize I wanted that same kind of love with my true soulmate. I also realized it was the magic of Christmas Mountain that made me wonder if finding my soulmate were possible.

It took me a little over an hour longer to put together the rest of the photographs, but eventually they were ready. I closed my laptop and checked the time on my cell phone. Was it too late to go upstairs and give it to Jacob now? I was excited to see the expression on his face when I surprised him but I didn't want to wake him if he was asleep.

I should definitely wait until tomorrow. That was the rational thing to do.

Two seconds later, I jumped to my feet and slipped out the door. I crept up the stairs with butterflies in my belly, feeling slightly ridiculous tiptoeing toward Jacob's attic apartment this late at night. The door to his apartment was closed this time. To my relief, I saw a light shining from beneath the door. Taking a deep breath, I knocked on the door quietly and then waited.

Rustling ensued from the other side of the door and a

few seconds later the door opened. Jacob stood there in a long-sleeve charcoal-colored waffle shirt with charcoal bottoms. His eyes widened and his mouth dropped open a little. Maybe this had been a dumb idea.

I started to turn around...

"Lacey!" he exclaimed, ending any chance that I'd willed myself invisible out of embarrassment. "What are you doing here?"

"At this late hour?" I asked, cringing.

"Yes. No," he said, suddenly a little flustered.

The corner of my mouth lifted. "If it's any consolation it's later in New York and now is when things really start up on a Friday night."

"Good to know," he said, chuckling as his shoulders relaxed. "This is a pleasant surprise. I just got home a little while ago from helping Mrs. Gallimore with her front door. It was sticking and she couldn't get out."

"No problems like that here," I joked.

"Would you like to come in?" he asked, a tiny line forming between his eyebrows.

I nodded, feeling shy as he stood back to let me pass. As Jacob shut the door, I glanced at the living area in the corner of the room, complete with couch and entertainment stand. My eyes widened when I saw that his TV was turned on.

"Well, well, well," I said, putting my laptop on the coffee table and turning to him with one hand on my hip. "Who would've thought Mr. Jacob Curtis *does* watch TV after all?!" I mocked good-naturedly, but Jacob's eyes widened and I had the feeling I'd said something wrong.

He made a grab for the remote control just as the commercial ended, and the theme tune for *Fourteen Days Till Forever* came on.

My mouth dropped open. "What the...?"

He held his hands up. "Busted."

"You're watching my show? Seriously?" I asked, feeling embarrassed. I loved helping contestants find love but these were fledgling relationships compared to Chuck and Nora or Betty and Randall Curtis. "You told me you hate these kinds of shows!"

"I, um . . ." He shrugged, not quite meeting my eye as he sat down, gesturing for me to join him on the couch. "I was just taking a quick look at the show to see what your work is all about and what might be in store for Christmas Mountain."

I narrowed my eyes at him and turned back to the TV. A beautiful brunette named Chantelle was riding a horse along a beach, her white chiffon scarf floating away on the ocean breeze and landing at the feet of a tall, dark, and handsome man named Byron, who picked it up and ran it through his hands before lifting it to his nose and inhaling the scent of Chantelle's perfume, his eyes closed in rapture.

"A quick look? This is the final episode of season three! Jacob Curtis, have you watched all three seasons of my show?" I asked, laughing with glee as I saw the stricken look on his face as he realized he'd been caught.

"Maybe this is the first episode I flipped to," he said tossing a pillow at me.

I caught the pillow, holding it out. "Here, you might need this to hide behind when you get all sentimental at the romantic scenes," I teased.

"Okay, I will take it." He shoved the pillow behind his head before shushing me so he could hear what was being said.

"You're shushing me so you don't miss anything?" I asked.

"Purely for research purposes" he said, consciously or

unconsciously mimicking a phrase I had used when I'd asked him about his love life.

"Research away," I said, sinking back into the sofa cushion.

We sat in silence as the scene unfolded. This couple had been one that hadn't worked out. I wished we were watching one of the earlier episodes. While my own love life had been seriously lacking, due to my work commitments—or, according to my ex, my unwillingness to trust anyone to take care of me—the loves and lives of the contestants had bridged that gap and given me the romance I had craved.

"Do you like this scene?"

He shrugged. "I don't want to criticize your work."

"Oh, come on. We get feedback all the time," I said, even though I found myself bracing for his feedback.

"Well, who rides a horse along a beach wearing a white dress like that?" he asked, his tone teasing. "And is that dude wearing matching white pants? They look like denim."

"Wardrobe picked them out!" I said, pulling the pillow out from under his head and hitting him on the arm with it.

"Ow!" he said, wearing a wide grin as he pulled his arm away. "You don't have to play rough. I'm just saying that jeans were invented for cowboys, right? Show me where in the history of the world, you've seen a cowboy spend days in the saddle wearing white jeans."

"Well it's a good thing *you* weren't wearing white when I first met you, or you'd have been impossible to find covered in the snow when you fell," I teased.

I might have taken offense to Jacob joking about my show, but I knew the man didn't have a mean bone in his body. Besides, I was enjoying the banter.

"Where was this one filmed again?" he asked, nodding at

the screen as Byron helped Chantelle off the horse, his hands gripping her tiny waist.

"The Big Island of Hawaii," I replied proudly.

"Do you think Hawaiians would wear that floaty and totally impractical dress on a horse ride?" he asked, laughing as I swatted him again.

"Hawaii is one of the most beautiful locations we've filmed," I said, wiping my eyes from laughing so hard. "We spent a day filming at the Akaka Falls and it was breathtaking. You must have seen it in episode three—"

"Two, it was in episode two," he said.

"Gotcha!" I grinned, loving his expression as he realized I'd said the wrong episode to get him to admit he'd watched all of the episodes.

"Very clever, Lacey," he said, slipping his arm around me. "Akaka Falls has nothing on Christmas Falls, though. I'll have to take you hiking up behind to Falls to show you what I mean."

"I'd love that," I said, a delicious shiver running up and down my spine.

The credits began to roll and with them came my favorite part, where we showed snippets from every episode which led up to the final moments of a couple's journey. We were sitting close together on Jacob's couch and I laid my head on his shoulder lost in the moment.

He put his hand on the back of my head, rubbing his fingers against my scalp gently. "I'm glad you came up here tonight."

"Me, too. . . That reminds me . . ." I sat up suddenly and grabbed my laptop. "I made something for you."

As the snapshots of the past few days flicked across my screen, Jacob fell silent, his expression growing serious as he took in each picture. He stopped the slideshow at the photo of his robin ornament in the shop window and zoomed in.

He turned to me. "You took a picture of that ornament I made?"

"I was drawn to it," I said, biting my bottom lip. "When I found out you made it I wasn't even surprised. It made total sense."

"Lacey . . ." He reached his hand out and brushed a strand of hair away from my face, tucking it behind my ear.

"Did you like the slideshow?" I asked.

"It's the nicest thing anyone has ever done for me," he whispered, before leaning close to me. He stopped with his mouth mere inches away from mine. "Thank you."

"You're welcome," I said, lifting my lashes and gazing up into those beautiful blue eyes.

Jacob's eyes searched mine and then ever-so-slowly he closed the distance between us and kissed me gently on the lips. My belly did a cartwheel and a warm blanket seemed to envelope me as he kissed me a second time, his mouth claiming mine with a little more urgency.

The theme tune of *Fourteen Days Till Forever* reached a crescendo in the background, alerting me that the last photos from the finale were about to be shown. The fans loved this segment the best.

I leaned back a little. "You're missing the best part," I whispered.

His gaze flicked toward the TV before returning to me. "No, I'm not. I'm concentrating on the best part right here . . . and she's not on the TV."

As Byron got down on one knee and proposed, I kissed Jacob again and again, without paying attention to the show. . . *my* show. Because a real-life romance was playing out away from the screen, and while this wasn't a reality show, it *was* reality—*my* reality—and as hard as I'd tried to fight them, there was no denying my feelings for Jacob anymore.

CHAPTER TWELVE

The next morning, I woke up to find a kink in my neck that so did *not* feel good. I opened my eyes, feeling confused as I blinked and took in the unfamiliar surroundings. A gentle, rhythmic sound came from somewhere above me and I lifted my head gingerly, mindful of the pain shooting down the left side of my neck.

My eyes flared as I realized what that sound was: Jacob's breathing. Twisting my head to look down (ouch!), I saw that my pillow—which had been surprisingly comfortable—was, in fact, Jacob's lap.

I sat up slowly with every intention of creeping out before Jacob woke up, but when I felt him stirring, I knew it was too late. I lifted my lashes and saw him looking down at me.

"Good morning, sleepyhead," he said.

"Morning," I said, putting a hand to my head to smooth my hair, which had to be a mess. "I'm sorry, but I must've fallen asleep while we were watching *To Kill a Mockingbird*."

He brushed my jawline with his finger. "Why do you have to be sorry for that?"

"This isn't exactly how I look my best."

"You look beautiful," he said, the corners of his mouth lifting. "Although, the way you cringed when you turned to look at me, I'm guessing it wasn't a comfortable night's sleep."

"Mmm . . ." I'd sleep on rocks to wake up like this next to him, but I wasn't going to admit that to him. Instead, I shook my head. "I was comfy. Just a little kink in my neck."

He reached down to rub at the knot in my neck muscle. "Here?"

"Mm-hmm," I said, clearly not into forming complete sentences this morning.

"After watching your show, I thought of some new locations last night. If you're free today, I was going to suggest showing you another place?"

"So, now you're okay with me filming here?"

He chuckled. "I didn't say that . . ."

"You must've loved the white pants more than I thought," I said, sitting up and stretching my neck. "That's a lot better. Thanks."

"My pleasure. What about the tour?"

"I'm free all weekend. I told my boss I'm not working this weekend. I even turned my phone off."

"Impressive," he said, tucking a piece of hair behind my ear. "That's new for you, right? As in, you *never* do that?"

I shrugged. "Well, you know what they say. All work and no play makes Lacey a dull girl."

"I can think of many words to describe you, Lacey Lane, but dull isn't one of them," he said.

My belly did a little flip. I opened my mouth to ask him what words he *would* use to describe me when he stood up and held his hand out.

"Let's meet downstairs in half an hour?" he asked, as I

put my hand in his. "We can get breakfast before heading out."

I nodded, standing. "Of course. Where are you taking me, anyway?"

He opened the door and stood back to let me out. "It's a surprise".

* * *

A quick shower later, I went downstairs, arriving at the door of the dining room to find Jacob waiting there for me. The dining room was empty and the table settings had already been set for lunch.

"Oh, no. We missed breakfast," I said, unable to believe I'd slept in so late. I always woke up early to maximize my work day.

"Not to worry." Jacob took my hand, steering me into the kitchen. "A perk of being the owners' son," he said, pushing open the door.

When we entered the kitchen, I saw a hive of activity. I stood spellbound at the festive and homey scene before me. Randall Curtis teetered on a stepladder in the corner of the room, while singing along to a Christmas carol blasting from a speaker. I put a hand to my cheek, hoping he didn't fall.

"Dad, I told you I'd do that," Jacob said, hurrying across the room.

"There you are," Mr. Curtis said, stepping down and handing his son a length of green and red tinsel, which featured tiny robins perched on holly branches.

"Got it." Jacob took the tinsel and climbed up a couple of steps.

Mr. Curtis smiled warmly at me. "Good morning, young

lady. Can I get you something? You've missed the cooked breakfast, I'm afraid, but there are plenty of pastries. My wife has been baking up a storm."

I shook my head, feeling embarrassed at being so late. "No, thank you, Mr. Curtis. It's my own fault I accidentally slept in."

Jacob gave me a look from across the room, making my cheeks heat.

"My wife wouldn't dream of letting a guest go hungry. Please, help yourself." He gestured to the table at the far end of the kitchen, which had pastries piled high on red plates.

The smell of cinnamon wafted into my nose, and I nodded, suddenly ravenous. I chose a cinnamon swirl and closed my eyes in delight as the still-warm pastry melted in my mouth.

Jacob finished hanging the tinsel and then joined me at the table, carrying two steaming mugs of coffee. I smiled gratefully at him before wrapping my hands around the cup as I took my first sip. I opened my mouth to ask him where he planned to take me today when the door opened and Ruby popped her head in.

She looked around the room and mouthed, "Mom?"

Jacob shook his head. "She's not here."

"Good!" Ruby pushed the door open wider and came in, carrying shopping bags. She plunked the bags onto the table and then pulled off her hat, shaking out her blonde hair. "It's freezing outside today, not literally but close! Ooh, cinnamon swirls, yum." She took a bite and rolled her eyes skyward in delight. "Just what I needed."

"Are those for me?" Mr. Curtis asked, nodding at the bags.

"Yep, you're welcome," Ruby said, giving him a smile.

He blew her a kiss, before turning to me. "Ruby is much

better at buying Christmas gifts than I am. I give her a vague idea and my credit card, and she does my shopping for me."

My eyes widened, surprised at how he'd just opened up to me about something so personal.

"Don't worry, Lacey," he said, chuckling. "Everyone knows Ruby does the choosing. I think they prefer it that way."

Jacob tried to peer into the bags. "Anything in there for me?" he asked.

Ruby fished around in one of the bags and pulled out a box, which she waved in front of her brother's face, before dropping it back in and moving the shopping bag out of Jacob's reach.

"Staying for breakfast, love?" Mr. Curtis asked.

Ruby shook her head. "Thanks, Dad. But Ribbons is still on the loose and I have got to find him. That dog will give me a heart attack one of these days."

"I'll help you look, Ruby," I offered, shooting Jacob an apologetic glance, but Ruby shook her head.

"Thanks Lacey, but I've got it. I know all his usual hideouts. It's just a case of figuring out which one he's holed up in. Everyone in town is used to his antics and I'm sure he's being fed and possibly housed." She took another bite of her cinnamon roll before reluctantly putting it back on the plate. "I'd better get to it. See you later."

We were enjoying the freshly baked pastries and hot steaming coffee when Mr. Curtis announced he was off in search of more decorations, leaving Jacob and me alone in the kitchen.

"Ruby doesn't live at the inn, does she?" I asked.

Jacob shook his head. "She owns a townhome. Her roommate is Morgan Reed, who owns the C.M. Salon on Main Street."

"Is she dating anyone?" I asked, curious to know why I hadn't seen her with anyone since I'd arrived.

He shook his head. "Too busy with work. Although I think she secretly has a crush on someone."

My ears perked up. "Who?"

He leaned closer. "Morgan's older brother. I've always sensed something between them, but so far . . . neither one has made a move," he said, shrugging.

"We should get the two of them on the show. Maybe I could spin it to Mel," I said, holding my hands up as if creating a frame. "Local couple finds love right where it's always been."

He laughed. "I don't think so."

"Then maybe *we* should go on the next season," I said, giving a little laugh to let him know I was joking. Kind of.

He leaned across the table until his face was inches from mine. "We don't need a show," he whispered and then lowered his lips to mine.

My heart melted and that same feeling of comfort washed over me. The kiss was soft and sweet, and his mouth tasted like cinnamon. Yum.

"Don't mind me, dears, just passing through," Betty said, as she sashayed past the dining room toward the kitchen.

I pulled back from Jacob and tried to hide behind my coffee mug, not sure which was hotter . . . the coffee or my cheeks after getting caught by Jacob's mom. How embarrassing. But he just chuckled, looking a little proud, which melted my heart even more.

CHAPTER THIRTEEN

Ruby was right . . . it *was* freezing outside. I was glad for my warm layers and Ruby's hiking boots, which she had told me to keep until I left Christmas Mountain since she had several other pairs. The snow was falling like thin white cotton puffs. I lifted my face to the sky, trying to catch a snowflake on my tongue.

Jacob laughed. "What are you doing?"

I didn't speak until a big snowflake landed on my tongue. I closed my eyes for a second or two before opening them and smiling at Jacob. "Making a wish."

"A wish?"

I held my arms wide. "You've never made a wish on a snowflake?"

He shook his head. "Never."

"Try it. It's fun," I said, sticking my tongue out again. "It's a tradition," I added, although it came out as 'ithu dadi-hun' because no matter how hard you may try, talking eloquently with your tongue sticking out was just not possible.

"Is it a New York thing?" he asked, the corners of his

mouth twitching. "It's definitely not a Christmas Mountain tradition."

"No, it's a . . ." I closed my mouth, trying to think about where I had first heard of it. A memory washed through my mind of my mom when I was young and still living with her. She showed me and said it's what all the cool kids did. Visions of us danced through my head. We were laughing and taking pictures as I spun around in the street outside the apartment with my arms outstretched and my tongue hanging out.

Jacob touched my arm yanking me from the vision in my head and I jumped.

"You all right, Lacey?" he asked.

"Hmm? Yes . . ." I tilted my head, wondering, not for the first time, where she might be and how she was doing. "I'm just . . . making wishes."

He took my face in his hands and kissed me gently. "What did you wish for?"

I buried my face in his cheek. "If I told you then it wouldn't come true. Don't you know anything about wishes?"

"I'm learning," he said, his fingers threading through my hair.

With one more kiss, we began walking again. Jacob held my hand. I loved how the world grew silent when it snowed; cars glided past soundlessly, and voices became muffled, as if the world were settling down under the cozy white blanket, which was covering everything. Even our footsteps were silent in the freshly fallen powder, the crunching of settled snow combining with all the other sounds.

I realized I was smiling to myself when my cheeks started to hurt. I opened my mouth wide to relax the muscles in my face.

"Are you trying to make a really big wish?" he asked, smiling.

I shook my head. "No, I'm just happy."

"I know the feeling." He gave me a side-glance and then looked straight ahead again. He clapped his gloved hands together. "Here we are," he said.

I stopped and looked up, and couldn't help feeling confused. The last place we visited together was The Sharing Tree, which had been so magical. So, the sight of Christmas Mountain Elementary School? Well, it was a pretty brick building, but school was not so exciting.

"This is what you wanted me to see?" I asked.

He nodded. "You wanted to see the *real* Christmas Mountain, so what better place to start than the place holding future generations?"

"Umm..."

He laughed. "What?"

"I didn't exactly love school as a kid. Just saying."

"Maybe that's because you weren't in Christmas Mountain," he said, his eyebrows lifting. "Give it a chance. They're having a dress rehearsal for the Christmas show today, and the entire town gets involved. It's one of the highlights of the year."

As he pulled open the double doors, a wave of noise hit me and I wondered how he thought the school would be relevant to a reality dating show. But, to be honest, I was a little bit curious to see the school where he'd grown up and it was the weekend, so I wasn't technically supposed to be working. We entered the building and found that the noise was coming from behind a second set of doors.

"Are you ready?" he asked.

I nodded, intrigued despite my bad memories of my own school days. Kids teasing me because my clothes were well-worn (and sometimes dirty). Never feeling like I belonged. Jacob pulled open the doors and a wave of noise washed over us. Actually, a wave makes it sound too gentle; the noise hit us like a sledgehammer. I winced, but as my ears adjusted to the high volume, I began to pick out individual sounds, the predominant one being laughter.

A little girl, who couldn't have been more than six years old, flung herself at Jacob and wrapped her arms around his legs. He laughed and ruffled her hair, and then bent to pick her up as he introduced us to each other.

"Mia, this is Lacey. Lacey, meet Mia."

The little girl looked at me with wide eyes, and reached out to touch my hair. "You're so pretty, and your hair looks like Dorothy's."

I blinked. "Is that a friend from school?"

"Wizard of Oz," Jacob supplied, watching me nod. "It's Mia's favorite movie ever, so take it as a supreme compliment."

"Well, thank you, Mia. Your hair is beautiful, too, like spun gold."

Mia giggled, and then wiggled out of Jacob's arms. Then she ran back to her teacher, who, I noticed, was blushing as she waved at Jacob. He seemed oblivious of the effect he had on girls young and older.

"She's adorable," I said.

"I went to school with her parents, who were high school sweethearts," Jacob said.

"Aww. How romantic," I said, thinking stories like this would be perfect to weave into the romantic history of Christmas Mountain. Oh, wait. I wasn't supposed to be thinking about work. Old habits seriously die hard.

Jacob led me toward the stage, where a glittering snow scene had been set up.

"The kids are doing a play which Miss Stecher wrote," he said, nodding in the direction of the pretty teacher who had waved to Jacob moments ago, and she blushed again. "It's about finding magic in the simplest of things."

I climbed up the stairs and onto the stage with him. "Sounds lovely."

He smiled at me, a strange look in his eyes which I couldn't quite fathom. Then he turned to the scenery and props on the stage. It was a beautiful set-up. The floor was a swathe of the softest white tulle, attached to a huge wooden board, and sprinkled with brilliant glitter that sparkled as the light caught it, just like the sun on freshly fallen snow.

Gently curved wooden shapes dotted the faux snow, painted white and covered in the same iridescent glitter as the floor. What seemed like a million tiny snowflakes were hung on strings which dangled from the ceiling, and off to the side of the stage was a child-sized sleigh, painted red and gold, with a sack of brightly wrapped gifts in the back.

As Jacob ran his hands critically over the curves of the wood, my first thought was *"Lucky wood"*, and my second was a realization that he had probably made this scenery himself.

The teacher clapped her hands, calling the children over. As if on cue, Jacob jumped off the front of the stage and held his hands up to help me down. As he held onto my waist and pulled me into his arms, I resisted the urge to kiss him, since we were surrounded by dozens of excited children. He nodded to the back of the school hall, and we stood and watched as the children filed up the stairs and onto the glittery stage in various outfits—some wearing woollen hats and scarves, others dressed as snowmen, and little Mia now dressed in a torn and tattered dress which made her look like little orphan Annie.

I opened my mouth to speak, but Jacob placed his finger gently to my lips and gestured to the stage as a piano struck up a few chords. Little Mia took center stage and began to sing, her voice really strong for someone so small.

I thought I was alone, with no place to call my home,
Until I found some friends who took me in,
With no mommy here to hold, I was feeling oh so cold,
But you've taught me that I'm safe to love again.

I felt a lump form in my throat. Mia's voice was so pure and beautiful that I teared up, but it was the words which really struck a chord in my heart. The other children, including the snowmen, all burst into a happy song, telling little orphan Mia that she was one of them now, and how home could be anywhere she feels loved.

After the song ended, Jacob and I clapped. Then Jacob waved to the teacher again before we walked outside, away from the heat of the school and back into the snow. I asked him if he'd helped with the decorations and he admitted that he had. He said the teacher was an old friend from school. Then he pulled a flask of hot chocolate from his backpack, along with a paper bag containing two of his mom's raspberry pastries from breakfast. We found a low wall and sat down next to each other, sharing the cocoa from one cup.

"That was a beautiful song. I know it's only make-believe but I wish I had found a circle of friends to take me in when I was a kid. It might have made me a different person, more trusting."

Jacob turned his head toward the sky and held his tongue out, trying to catch a snowflake.

I laughed. "What are you doing?"

"Making a wish," he said, before leaning in and kissing the tip of my nose.

"I thought you didn't believe in my little ritual?" I teased.

He nodded back toward the school. "You can find magic in the simplest of things," he said, echoing the theme of the school play.

I picked up a pile of snow and began rolling it into a ball. "Can I tell you a secret? I don't really believe in magic. I believe that some people are destined to find love, and others aren't."

He took my hand. "That's a sad thought. Let me tell *you* a secret."

"What?" I asked.

"I *do* believe in magic."

My eyes watered. "You do?"

He nodded. "I believe there's enough love in this world for everyone." He leaned down and kissed me gently on the lips. "Especially for you."

I closed my eyes and nuzzled into his neck. "What about you, Jacob?"

"Me?" he asked.

"Mmhmm."

"I've always believed I would have the same love story as my parents. Anything else is unacceptable. I've waited all these years knowing you . . ." He paused and cleared his throat. Then his voice dropped to a whisper as he said, "Knowing the right woman would come along when the time was right."

My belly did a flip. Did he mean that I was the right woman for him?

I bit my bottom lip. "I admire your faith. I've been independent for so long that the thought of depending on someone else terrifies me."

He brushed a strand of hair away from my face. "And yet you produce a show where couples find each other and fall in love?"

I nodded. "That's true for them. Actually, only for some of them like you pointed out. But that doesn't mean it would happen in my life."

He eased off the wall until he stood in front of me, cupping my face. "What am I going to do with you?"

I looked into his eyes. "Me?"

He nodded, his expression softening. "Something happened to me the moment I first looked up at you from a pot of poinsettias.

My heart fluttered. "You wanted to knock me off a ladder as payback?"

The corner of his mouth lifted. "That sounds fun."

"Hey!" I said, swatting him playfully on the arm.

"It was your idea," he said, chuckling. Then he touched my cheek. "But, seriously. You remember that first day at the inn when we were talking by the window? And I disappeared."

My stomach knotted. "You said you had something you had to deal with."

He nodded, sucking in a deep breath. "My feelings."

I tilted my head. "I don't understand."

"My dad has always told me it was love at first sight for him with my mom, but I never truly understood what that meant. It had never happened to me. Until that day."

My eyes watered. "When you ghosted me, I thought that meant you didn't like me."

"Quite the opposite only . . . it took me by surprise," he said, cupping my face with his hands. "You're my Nora," he said, simply.

Okay, that was it. A tear slipped down my cheek and there was nothing I could do about it.

I sniffled. "You want to talk about surprises? I've never felt like I belonged anywhere until I came to this tiny mountain town. You and everyone I've met here have all been a surprise . . . no, a *shock* to me."

"Why?" he asked, pulling me against him and clasping his arms around me.

My heart squeezed. "I've been alone so long I didn't want to risk getting my heart broken."

"Lacey, I would never hurt you," he said, his voice firm.

"You can't say that for sure, Jacob. People get their hearts broken all the time," I said, knowing I couldn't really count on him unless I wanted to take that risk. "How do you know I won't break your heart?"

A line formed between his eyebrows. "I guess I don't."

"Well, then," I said, starting to take a step back but he held me tight.

"I'll tell you one thing, though," he said, his eyes peering into mine. "If I didn't give this everything, I know I'd live to regret it. I've completely fallen for you, Lacey."

Sirens blared in my head. Everything in me screamed that I should run now and run fast.

"I've fallen for you, too," I said, my world spinning and his arms holding me steady. "I'm also falling for your family." I lifted my lashes and looked into his eyes. "Is that silly?"

"No, it isn't." He shook his head and pulled me close to him, caressing my hair. He rested his cheek on top of my head. "I think they feel the same way about you."

I stayed with my cheek against his soft jacket, letting him stroke my hair as all kinds of warnings sounded through my head.

This could never work.

I was a city girl.
He was a small-town guy.
We lived completely different lives and in different states.

I sucked in a deep breath. While Jacob's optimism was lovely to hear, I couldn't believe in a happy-ever-after for me. I'd been abandoned before and it had been so hard to push through that loneliness and build a life on my own. If things didn't work out between us and I lost him, lost his wonderful family, then it would crush me. But he sounded so certain that I didn't want to tell him how I felt. For a moment, at least, I wanted to pretend he was right.

CHAPTER FOURTEEN

The next day, I needed time and space to clear my head. After Jacob and I had revealed our feelings to each other, my mind spun and I couldn't concentrate on anything—a fact which was demonstrated when I spent thirty minutes trying to straighten my hair, only to find I hadn't switched on the flattening iron. Sigh.

I had the urge to escape into work, but reminded myself I was supposed to be taking the weekend off and it was Sunday. Okay, I'd compromise and wait until the afternoon. Carol had called me last night to say the book club was meeting today, which was perfect. Right now, what I really needed was some girl time.

The freezing cold felt like an anesthetic, both to my confusion and to my toes. By the time I reached Rudolph's Reads, I literally could not feel my feet. Brrr.

As I pushed open the front door the same raucous laughter hit me as before, making me smile. This was going to be exactly what I needed. I wasn't quite at the stage where I felt I could confide in the other girls, but girl talk sounded plentiful in the back room of Carol's bookstore.

"Lacey, you're here!" Carol stood up when I entered the back room and reached across the chairs to give me a hug. Then she gestured for me to take the only empty chair. The book club was certainly popular.

"Hot cider, anyone?" Nina called, brandishing a ladle.

"I'd love some, thanks." I settled down in the chair and gratefully accepted the mug of hot cider Nina handed to me. Wrapping my hands around the mug, I sniffed deeply, closing my eyes at the spicy scent.

"It's a good thing Harmony didn't make the cider or you'd be intoxicated just from the fumes," Nina joked, as Harmony rolled her eyes before taking a sip from her cup.

"Might as well be drinking apple juice with this," Harmony said, chuckling in retaliation. "How's yours, Lacey?"

I took a sip, the warm spicy liquid rolling across my tongue and then warming my throat. "It's delicious. Best cider I've ever had," I said, truthfully.

"Do you still go out to any of our fun hot spots in New York, Lacey?" Carol asked.

I shook my head. "Once filming is over for the day, I'm usually exhausted and my favorite thing to do is hit the sack."

"And wake up with the sound of the Pacific Ocean in your ears, if I remember last season correctly," Harmony said, sounding as enthusiastic as when I first met her. Her blonde hair was brushed back from her face and she leaned forward in her chair, wiggling her eyebrows as if waiting for my reply.

I laughed. "Well, I have seen some pretty awesome places, yes. But seriously, I don't think any of them can compare to Christmas Mountain."

I was half expecting them all to mumble something

along the lines of 'oh it's ok I suppose, but I'd really like to visit such and such', but they all nodded in agreement. They clearly loved their town. And who wouldn't?

"Which of our attractions has drawn you in the most?" Giselle, the writer asked, watching me closely with a mischievous glint in her eyes.

"I loved The Sharing Tree. It's very moving and the sound of the waterfall only adds to the magic."

The girls looked at one another, grinning.

My eyebrows lifted. "What did I miss?"

"I think they mean more along the lines of a certain person, rather than a place, Lacey," Carol said, giving me a meaningful look.

All heads swiveled in my direction, and I felt my cheeks heat. "Oh, I see. . . Well, I've been so busy working that I've not really had time to meet many people."

Knowing smiles ensued, and then, to my relief, Carol changed the subject.

"Okay, so who wants to start the book business off today? Macy? Have you got any recommendations for our next read?"

As the conversation turned to all things literary, I breathed a sigh of relief. On the one hand, I might welcome the girls' advice about Jacob. After all, many of them had probably known him most of their lives. But on the other hand, I didn't want them thinking I was some out-of-towner having a fling with a local guy.

Macy held up a book with a picture of a hot pink stiletto on the cover, and the girls sent up a collective 'wooooo' and made comments about it looking rather sexy. I sat listening to them, grinning at the good-natured teasing that was going on around the room.

A blast of cold air suddenly drifted under the door,

followed swiftly by Ruby, looking a little red in the face and slightly miffed.

"Hi, Ruby," Carol said. "What's up?"

"It's Ribbons," she said.

"Has he gone AWOL again?" Carol asked.

"Yes," Ruby said.

"I swear, that dog is the best escape artist I have ever known," Carol said, shaking her head. "When did he bolt?"

Ruby accepted the mug of cider that Nina held out and then took a sip, before unwinding her scarf from around her neck and blowing out her cheeks.

"Oh, hey, Lacey," she said, seeming to notice me for the first time. "Always fun to see you."

My heart warmed. "Thanks, Ruby."

Turning back to Carol, she said, "Ribbons bolted the same day Lacey arrived in town. That's why I couldn't show Lacey around. I had to ask Jacob to give her the tour so I could go look for that mischievous dog."

"I'm sorry you haven't found him yet," I said, biting my bottom lip.

"How sad," Giselle said. "You love that dog, Rubes."

Ruby nodded. "I do, that's why I'm running around all over town looking for him. Never mind a leash, that dog needs a padlock and chain to keep him safe."

"Hey, do you remember when Rudy went missing last year? Now *that* was a search and rescue mission if ever I saw one," Harmony said, shaking her head, grinning at the memory.

I frowned. "Rudy?"

Harmony nodded. "Yeah, his name is short for Rudolph. He's the lead reindeer from Silver Bells and he wandered off one day. We had practically the whole town looking for him."

"Silver Bells? That's the luxury tour business, right? I was planning on heading up there this afternoon to check it out. What's it like?"

"It's magical," Giselle said. "You should get . . . *someone* . . . to take you on one of their sleigh rides. You'll go through this winter wonderland and end up at Santa's Grotto—"

"And you get to eat real cookies baked by the elves, too!" interrupted Harmony.

I narrowed my eyes, not sure if they were pulling my leg or not.

Giselle seemed to notice my confusion and laughed. "Seriously, we all love the tour and we get together every Christmas and go up there for a girls' day out. It wouldn't be Christmas without a trip to see Santa in his grotto."

"Interesting . . ." I smiled and then noticed Ruby out of the corner of my eye. Her brow crinkled and she wore a faraway expression. I put an arm around Ruby. "Don't worry, Ruby. Ribbons will turn up. You said he always does, right? Like you said before, that St. Bernard is most likely fast asleep in front of someone's fire right at this moment, waiting for you to find him and take him home again."

"Thanks, Lacey," Ruby said, giving me a weary look.

I made a mental note to ask Jacob if he would take me over to Silver Bells before I left. Maybe we could go when I wasn't busy working, so I could enjoy the sleigh ride as a tourist and not as a producer. I sat back, and a warm glow washed through my chest. I was pretty sure it wasn't from the delicious cider, either.

I'd never been a part of anything in my life. I'd never had a family and I'd never had a close group of friends, either. Between Jacob and his family, and the book club, though, I was really starting to feel like . . . well, like I belonged. A knot formed in my belly at the thought that I'd be leaving soon and this would all end.

* * *

"Sorry ladies, but we've run out of time for book club today and I know some of you have other things to get done before the weekend ends," Giselle said, lifting up the trade paperback book with the hot pink stiletto on the cover. "If we're all in agreement, we'll read Macy's choice, *Shoe and Tell*. Should be cute, Macy. We're a high-brow book club here."

Macy laughed. "It's a sweet romance novel, about a shoemaker and a rich woman who usually wears designer heels, but can't find the perfect pair so asks the shoemaker to make her a unique pair."

"And let me guess, *they* end up being the beautiful pair, instead?" Giselle teased.

At the mention of shoes, I shivered. I remembered Jacob holding my ankle gently while he fitted my foot into the ice skate. My thoughts were distracted by a persistent rapping sound coming from the front of the store.

Carol stuck her head around the door, said something to the person who was out there, and then closed the door again. "It's Jacob Curtis."

"Woo-wooo!" the gals sang in unison. "Lacey..."

I bit my bottom lip. These girls certainly did their share of 'woooing'! "What makes you think he's here for me? Maybe he wants to see his sister."

"Nice try, but he asked if you were here and what time the book club finished," Carol said.

My heart did a little flip. "Oh..."

"He said he'd wait outside for you," Carol said, her eyes

lighting up as she rubbed her hands together. "He said he has a surprise for you."

"Woooo!" the gals sang again.

"I wonder what that could be," I said, shaking my head at them although I couldn't help but smile. I gathered my coat and purse, kissed Carol on the cheek, and then said goodbye to everyone else. I hurried to the door, banging my hip painfully on the countertop in my hurry.

Oops. So much for if I wanted to appear nonchalant.

I saw Jacob through the window and my belly danced. A pang of regret soon followed because I'd be heading back to the city soon and leaving him behind. My steps slowed as I approached the window and I studied him while he was looking the other way. As usual, faded jeans clung to his long, muscular legs, and a thick, padded black jacket hugged his frame, the collar turned up against the cold, a navy-blue beanie on top of his blond hair. He was scraping snow from the sidewalk. He looked so handsome it was hard to believe he was my . . . what? Not my boyfriend since I was leaving soon. Was he just a guy I was seeing? That didn't feel right either. What a mess.

The door tinkled as I opened it. "Hey, Jacob."

He smiled. "Hey. I hope I didn't interrupt anything . . ."

"No, it's fine. We were just wrapping up."

He nodded. "Oh, good."

"Um, Carol said you had a surprise for me?" I asked.

He threw his arms wide. "Ta-da . . . I'm the surprise! Well?"

I raised an eyebrow at him. "For real?"

He grinned. "Okay, I'm not the actual surprise."

"You don't have to bring me a surprise," I said, shaking my head.

"Good to know," he said, putting his hands in his front

pockets and suddenly looking a little shy. "What are you up to this afternoon? Any plans?"

I'd meant to work, but with Jacob here in front of me I tilted my head. "No plans that are set in stone. Actually, I was thinking of heading up to Santa's Grotto. I need to find more locations for the show, and that sounds like a good contender."

"Santa's Grotto is a cherished tradition in this town, but we've missed their last tour for today. But I have the next best thing . . ." he paused for dramatic effect. "How about *this*? Surprise!"

I watched as he pulled something from behind his back and I gasped. It was the sled that I had helped him with the other night in his workshop in the attic apartment. Butterflies danced in my belly at the memory of him holding my hands and gliding them along the wood.

"Wow, Jacob. You finished it. It's so beautiful."

He looked ridiculously pleased at my excitement and he set it down on its runners, holding onto the red and green plaited rope, which was tied to the front.

"I think it's my best one yet. So, how about we combine business with pleasure and take the sled just north of Santa's Grotto? There are some great runs up there which are perfect for sledding, and it just so happens that your tour guide for the afternoon—aka *yours truly*—is an expert sledder. You'll be in very safe hands." He raised his eyebrows as he said the last sentence, and a delicious shiver ran down my spine.

"That sounds wonderful." I laughed and clasped my hands together. "Okay, but I really do have to get some work done."

"I thought you were taking the weekend off," he said.

"My phone has been off since Friday night and now it's

Sunday afternoon. Trust me, that is me taking the weekend off. But I'm itching to do a little more research, so I don't get fired."

"Well, that sounds good." He slipped his arm around my shoulder as we began to walk. "If you get fired then you won't have to go back to the city and you can stay here in Christmas Mountain. It's not a bad place to live, you know. Ask any of us townsfolk."

"Oh, really?" I joked, the thought of living here flitting through my mind. "So, if I up and move, I'd definitely be fired. Then what would I live on? I wouldn't have a job, remember?"

He cast his eye over the sled. "You could be my chief sled maker."

I gave him a side-glance. "Are you going to pay me in Prancer's Pancakes?"

"Done deal."

"Now there's an offer I can't refuse." I laughed, relieved that the conversation had stayed on a lighthearted level. I wanted to enjoy the afternoon without any angst, and I was afraid that if we began to seriously discuss me going home, I might break out in tears.

Jacob offered to drive us to the sledding spot but I preferred to walk, so we set off toward the mountain, stopping every now and again so that I could take photos and videos to send back in my next report to Mel. It wasn't an easy hike though, and having not been in the gym for a couple of weeks meant that my leg muscles were soon aching.

"Oh, wow," I gasped, bending over to catch my breath. "Is it much further? We must have scaled the equivalent of Kilimanjaro by now."

Jacob smiled. "Maybe halfway there? A bit less? I did offer to drive, Ms. Independent."

I nodded, still trying to catch my breath. "Well, you should have insisted, thrown me over your shoulder or something. I was *not* prepared for this." ·

I closed my eyes to take a deep breath and suddenly the ground fell away from my feet as Jacob flung me over his shoulder, fireman style.

"Like this?" he called to me.

"No, no, I take it back!" I laughed, kicking my legs to no effect, with yelps of *I'm going to break your back* in between giggles.

To his credit, Jacob carried me for quite a way before lowering me back to firm ground. A few minutes later, we were surrounded by deep green fir trees, their branches heavy with yesterday's snow, and the winter sun caused the ice to sparkle like diamonds.

"Okay, I think it's time to take this baby for a test run. Are you up for it?" Jacob turned the sled so that it was facing back down the way we had just trekked

"I'm game, but keep in mind I'm a newbie," I said.

He took his seat at the back, patting the bench in front of him. I was nervous, but the thought of gliding silently down the snow-covered mountain with Jacob's arms wrapped around me was too tempting to turn down, so I grinned and sat down in between his strong thighs.

"Ready?" His lips were close to my ear and I shivered. If I turned my face to the left then I could kiss him if I weren't so terrified about the sled ride.

"As ready as I'll ever be," I managed to get out and I swear I heard him chuckle.

"Okay, here we go." He pushed against the ground with his boot-clad feet and the sled inched forward. He pushed again and again before the incline got steeper and we picked up speed. I squealed as the trees sped past us, feeling equally terrified and exhilarated. I leaned back into Jacob's strong chest as he skillfully steered us downhill, using the ropes he held in his hands.

"We're turning, so lean into it, Lacey. Don't try and straighten up."

"Okay!" I nodded, the cold air rushing against my cheeks as he maneuvered us to the left. Every instinct told me to try and correct the balance and I leaned too far the other way. The sled careened out of control and flipped over, sending Jacob and me flying through the air.

I landed in the snow with a thud that winded me. It took me a few seconds to realize we were no longer flying on the sled. I sat up slowly, feeling slightly dazed.

"Lacey? Are you all right?" Jacob's voice held an urgent tone, so I scrambled to my feet, worried that he was hurt.

But when I saw him, my eyes widened. Jacob had been flung close to a tree and, by some fluke, his belt loop had snagged itself onto the end of a branch, rendering him unable to move.

"Um, are you okay?" I asked.

He grinned. "Just hanging out."

I bent over and laughed so hard that tears rolled down my face.

Eventually, I managed to unhook him, still laughing, and he began to chase me through the snow. I screamed and ran, very inelegantly, until I tripped on the sled rope and fell. Jacob flung himself onto the snow beside me.

I rolled over so that I was facing him, loving the huge grin on his face. He pushed himself up onto his elbows and gently wiped some snow off my nose. I reached up to do the same and our eyes met, his traveling slowly down to my lips before he lowered his face to mine. Our mouths touched, ever so gently, when I heard strange heavy breathing coming from behind me.

"What the . . .?" Jacob yelled, as a shower of snow engulfed us, followed by two giant hairy paws which pinned Jacob onto his back.

"It's a dog," I exclaimed, rolling away from the chaos to safety.

"Ribbons! There you are," Jacob said, as the huge St. Bernard licked his face joyfully.

CHAPTER FIFTEEN

"My goodness, this dog is heavy," I said, grunting, as Jacob and I tried to coax Ribbons up the path to the front door of the inn.

"And stubborn," Jacob said, pushing Ribbons' furry backend while I tried to lead him by the collar. "I might suggest to Ruby that she lets the clippers slip the next time she grooms him. He'd be a ton lighter without all . . . this . . . shaggy . . . fur."

At that moment, Ribbons decided to sit right there in the snow outside the front door, and Jacob had to literally lift the dog up onto his legs again.

"Maybe he's just tired, poor thing," I said.

Jacob gave me a look. "Tired? More like stuffed full of pastries from someone's kitchen where he's been hiding out. No one can resist his big puppy dog eyes, so they give him treats all the time."

"Aww. Are you upset because you have competition for being the sweetest guy in town?" I teased, laughing and then screaming as Ribbons chose that moment to shake, sending a cloud of powdery snow all over me.

"That's what you get for being cute," he retorted.

"You think I'm cute?" I asked, fluttering my eyelashes.

Jacob opened his mouth just as the front door opened and Ruby appeared in the doorway.

"Ribbons!" she exclaimed. "Where have you been hiding?"

"Wait," I said, as Ruby moved as if she were about to run out into the snow in her socks. I grabbed Ribbons' collar again and began to lead him toward her.

"It's okay, Ruby, we've got this. You'll get frostbite if you come out without shoes."

"It's fine, *I've* got this. Ribbons, c'mere boy," she said, hurrying toward him.

Ribbons took one look at her and turned tail, bounding up the street, looking back every few steps to see if she was following him in this new, fun game.

"Ribbons!" we all cried at the same time, which just made the dog wag his tail even harder.

"We'll go after him, sis. You don't have your boots on," Jacob said, holding out his hand for the leash Ruby was holding.

"No," she said, pushing his hand away, slipping on a pair of boots as she started to move in Ribbons' direction. Her eyebrows came together. "It's my problem. I'll deal with it."

Jacob watched her run off and then shrugged. "And we thought Ribbons was stubborn. He's got nothing on my sister," he said, giving me a look.

I grimaced. "I guess it's hard to ask for help sometimes."

"What should we do now?" he asked.

I pulled off my gloves and blew into my hands. Now that we'd stopped moving, I was getting cold. "How about a coffee?" I suggested.

His eyes lit up. "Are you asking me on a date?"

"If that's what it takes to get you there. You. Me. Coffee," I said, loving how we always teased each other. "Date."

"Well, when you put it like that the invitation is irresistible," he said, putting a hand to his heart.

I laughed. "Good. Let's go."

Jingle Bells Bakery was packed when we arrived, as it so often seemed to be, so we decided to get our coffees to go. While standing in line I stomped my feet to keep them warm.

"Are you still cold? Do you want my jacket?" Jacob asked.

I shook my head, touched by his offer. "No, but thank you. You need it as much as I do."

"I'm a mountain man, remember? I'm made of stronger stuff than the city types you're used to." He flexed his biceps comically, and I couldn't help but swoon a tiny bit as I imagined his arms around me.

I opened my mouth to come back with a witty retort about how he needed a long beard to be a mountain man—

"Jacob Curtis! Oh, my goodness. How *are* you?" a woman said.

Jacob spun around and a smile spread across his face. "Hi, Miranda."

If he intended to say anything else, it was lost in the shoulder of a very trendy skiing jacket as a woman flung her arms around his neck and pulled him close. Miranda was tall and slender, with four-inch heels on her boots.

I took a step back, suddenly feeling small and invisible. To make matters worse, I was next in line, and with Jacob so absorbed in his, um, *friend*, I didn't know what he wanted to drink. I played it safe and ordered two Christmas Bunnies (aka: vanilla lattes) to go, and then stood there feeling foolish as I waited for her to finish gushing over him.

Finally, Jacob stepped back. "Lacey, this is an old friend, Miranda. Miranda, this is Lacey."

Miranda held her hand out, so self-assured that not a hint of jealousy would even have entered her mind. "Old *girl*friend, he means, although less of the old if you don't mind, Jakey. Lacey is a pretty name."

Jakey? Old Girlfriend? Obviously, I knew he'd had girlfriends in the past, and it wasn't even as if they were still a thing, but still, that green eyed woman sure seemed threatening.

"Thanks." I smiled, shook her hand, and then handed Jacob his coffee. "I got you a Christmas Bunny. I wasn't sure what you wanted as you were *busy*," I said, my stomach clenching. "I'm going to head back to the inn. Nice to meet you, Miranda."

"You too," she said, waving.

"Wait up, Lacey." Jacob turned to Miranda, and kissed her on the cheek. "I have to go. We should catch up sometime."

As he moved in my direction, Miranda grabbed hold of his arm. "How about tomorrow night? I don't have any plans, and it would be awesome to spend some time together. Alone. We could go to our favorite place, remember?" she asked.

I waited for Jacob to say thanks, but, no thanks.

Instead, he said, "Sure, fine."

Miranda blew him a kiss, waved at me, and then walked off in the opposite direction.

* * *

Jacob caught up with me down the sidewalk in a few long strides and fell into step beside me. "Thanks for the coffee, I needed this."

"You needed it?" I asked.

He took a sip. "Sure. Even mountain men get cold."

My eyebrows came together. "Oh."

He looked at me quizzically. "Are you okay?"

I nodded. "Yes, I'm fine."

"Okay," he said, his brow creasing. "Should we take a walk to the bench?"

I shrugged and crossed the street toward Chuck and Nora's seat. Feeling a hundred shades of jealous, I sat down and took a long sip of my drink.

He sat next to me. "What are you doing?"

I shrugged. "Well, usually one sits on a bench when one walks to it."

The corners of his mouth twitched. "This is true. But I was actually talking about Kissing Bench up by The Sharing Tree. Not Chuck and Nora's Bench by the side of Main Street."

"Oh," I said.

"Shall we?" He held his hand out, pulling me to my feet and then taking my empty cup from me. He jogged across the street to put our empty cups in the trash. Then he returned to my side and we walked in silence once again, although I did catch him giving me the side-eye a few times. But I couldn't tell him how I really *hated* the idea of him going to dinner with his ex-girlfriend. She was just way too pretty.

Jealous much, Lacey?

Yeah, well, I couldn't help it.

Miranda had a past with Jacob and she could potentially have a future with him since she was oh-so-conveniently located in the same town, unlike yours truly. I let out a long breath. We walked in silence down the street and up the stairs to the bench, mainly because I was out of breath from trying to keep up with his long strides. A mutinous voice in my head told me that Miranda would have no problem keeping up with him with her long legs.

Still, as soon as we got there, I felt my mood lift a little. The sound of the Falls soothed my soul, and The Sharing Tree tinkled and sparkled in the cold winter breeze. Every branch was literally filled with love, and the gentle but powerful energy felt palpable.

We sat down and I sighed, stretching my legs out in front of me.

"That was a big sigh."

I smiled. "I just love this place. It calms me. Does that sound silly?"

He shook his head. "Not at all. I've often come up here to clear my head."

"I can see why," I said, wanting to press him for more information about Miranda. Inwardly, I argued that their relationship was in the past, yet they were seeing each other tomorrow night which was in the future. Finally, my curiosity got the best of me since it's not like I was a saint. "So, tell me about Miranda."

"Not much to tell. We dated for a while right after college. But she was never satisfied living in a small town—a backwater, as she called it. In fact, she was never satisfied with much of anything." He sighed. "Or anyone."

"Huh," I said, finding it hard to believe any woman couldn't be satisfied with Jacob.

"She had hopes for life in the big city, so she began spending more and more time away from Christmas Mountain. A weekend here, a week there. Don't get me wrong, she's a lovely person and things between us were great for a time but..."

"But what?"

He shrugged. "It wasn't enough. I starting spending more time on my crafts and she had higher aspirations. We went our separate ways, amicably."

"How could she not love it here?" I asked, sitting back and looking around me. I took in the beautiful mountain, the town that felt like home, and the warm people I'd met, and wondered what else there was to want.

He took my hand. "Well, some people prefer the big glamorous career and the bright lights of the city, right?"

"I suppose," I said, my stomach churning. "So, how did it end?"

He shrugged. "She gave me an ultimatum: Christmas Mountain or her. And the rest, as they say, is history."

My eyes welled. "Did you ever regret your choice?"

"Never," he said, shaking his head. "She and I had a good time. We cared a lot about each other, but if she'd been the right person for me then she would have been content with Christmas Mountain, and with me. But she wasn't, which suited me fine once I got over the initial heartbreak. I can't imagine wanting to live anywhere else."

"Did you even consider moving to the city for her?" I asked, knowing that this question seemed like madness since I would be returning to New York soon.

"Not seriously." He turned to me, his eyes searching mine. I thought for a moment he was going to kiss me. Instead, he shook his head. "This is my home."

Ouch. I cringed.

"There were other things that were wrong with our relationship. When I looked at my parents, or Chuck and Nora, I see what real love is . . . easier than what she and I had.

Obviously, there are those times when you have to work at the relationship. I'm not saying it's always going to be smooth sailing. But the *good* times should just flow without being filled with ultimatums and demands and drama. If you know what I mean?"

"Yes, I do."

He looked at me, a wry smile on his face. "What about you? Tell me about your life and loves in the Big Apple."

I laughed. "Well, loves . . . there's not much to tell. Or rather, *nothing* to tell. I've never had a relationship that lasted more than a few months."

"Why not?"

"Work has been my priority. I get my romance through the show. I love it, getting to create these opportunities and then watching love blossom between two people. It makes me happy to see their dreams come true."

"What about your dreams?" he asked, squeezing my hands.

The light and bright studio apartment flashed into my mind. "I've always dreamed of owning my own place. I know most people rent in the city and I rent now. But I want . . . no, I *need* the security of owning my own apartment."

"That's your dream?"

"Yes," I said, squeezing his hand. "For as long as I can remember, there has been this ache in my chest, or this worry, about being kicked out and having to move. Probably from moving so much as a kid and I'm over having to move anymore."

"I can understand that," he said, slipping his arm around me and pulling me closer to him.

I leaned my head on his shoulder. "I've been saving for a down payment, so I can buy something. Somewhere I know I'll never have to leave. A place to call home."

Jacob was silent, making me wonder what he was thinking.

"If this location gets approved for filming then my bonus will be enough to buy my dream," I said, tears burning my eyes. "I've worked so hard to get to this point. I've pulled more all-nighters than I can even count, but it will be worth it for that security."

He lifted my chin. "Lacey..."

"I've never had that before," I admitted, gazing into those deep, soulful eyes. "I've never been in a home which was secure. Every time I got used to one home, to one family, I was moved on to another home and another family. I have no parents, no one who loves me."

"You do now," he said, so quietly that I wasn't even sure if I'd heard him correctly. "I love you, Lacey."

My heart fluttered in my chest. Okay, there was no mistaking what he said now. When I saw that tender look in his eyes, I knew I hadn't been imagining things either.

"I love you, too," I whispered, lifting my chin. "I love everything about who you are, even that you don't want my show filmed here."

"How can you say that?" he asked, blowing out a breath.

I leaned toward him, my mouth a mere whisper from his. "Because it's part of who you are."

He caressed my cheek. "I feel awful knowing now that your dream depends on it."

Something niggled, but I couldn't figure out what it was. And, to be honest, at this moment I didn't really care. All I wanted was one thing. I leaned forward and kissed the man I'd fallen for. Despite the cold weather, the kiss was tender and sweet. The little hole in my chest felt a rush of thick warmth and then the hole vanished, leaving my chest radiating with joy.

We kissed for a long time until the shuffle of feet pulled us apart. A woman cleared her throat as she walked by holding another woman's hand, and the two exchanged knowing smiles. Oops. I'd been lost in the moment and had forgotten we were in public. I wanted to protest that it *was* called Kissing Bench, after all.

The couple hung ornaments on the tree and then moved further up the path, stopping near the Falls to lean against the railing.

I turned back to Jacob, who shrugged. "I'd do it all over again," he said.

"You're terrible," I joked, sitting back in the bench and putting my hand in his. "I'm sorry, Jacob. The fact that I live in New York City must be like déjà vu for you after what happened with Miranda."

He shrugged. "I wasn't enough for her. I don't blame her, never have."

"I can't believe she would let you go," I said, thinking aloud.

He smoothed a wisp of hair away from my face. "Thanks for the compliment."

I closed my eyes at his touch, wanting to kiss him again, but resisting.

"So, on your show, you have 'moments', right?" Jacob said, lifting his hands and gesturing. "At certain points in the scene, the 'moment' pops up with a caption and says 'how embarrassing' or the 'be still my beating heart' moment, right?"

"Yes." I nodded, touched that he'd remembered.

"What would you call this moment?" he asked.

I raised my eyebrows. "You mean us? Right now?"

"Right," he said, the corner of his mouth hitching

upward. "How would you caption that, professionally speaking?"

My face broke into a smile. "Hmm... I'd have to call it the 'My toosh is numb from sitting on a frozen bench' moment."

He shook his head. "Seriously, though. If we were in your show, and two of the cast—"

"Contestants. Cast makes it sound like it's a set-up," I corrected.

He bowed his head slightly. "Apologies. If this was a scene from the show filmed here and two of the *contestants* had just opened up to each other, what would you call it?"

I closed my eyes to think. "I'd call it 'The Sharing Tree' moment."

"Not bad," Jacob said, standing up. He walked over to the tree and touched one of the branches, the one that held the snow boots ornament I'd put on the tree. "Do you remember what you hung this ornament for?"

"Yes, I remember." I stood, walked over to him, and slipped my arms around his neck. Then I took a deep breath for courage. "I hung the ornament for the promise of finding the one person I could love and trust."

"Lacey, do you think...?"

Whatever he was going to say was lost as I pressed my lips to his. We sank into a tender kiss that made my legs weak as his arms circled my waist. As Jacob held me in his arms, the worry of being alone fell off my shoulders and drifted away on the cool breeze.

This moment was perfect, with the sound of the waterfall behind us, the tinkling of the ornaments, and the low throb of a Hummer. Wait, what?

My eyes snapped open and I spun around, just as a shiny black Hummer limo pulled up to the bottom of the steps. A driver jumped out and hurried around to the rear passenger side to open the door. A pair of blue snakeskin cowboy boots crunched into the snow as they emerged from the car and my heart sank.

"Mel?" I called out. With a quick glance at Jacob, I hurried down the steps.

"Careful, it's slick," Jacob said, descending at the same pace beside me.

My boss stepped from the car, with a ridiculously expensive-looking furry coat around his shoulders and a fat cigar hanging from his lip.

"Mel?" Jacob asked, hopping off the last step beside me.

"My boss," I said, every nerve in my body going on red alert.

Mel looked from me to Jacob and then back to me again. "You're alive, then?"

"You prefer sunshine and sangria," I said, unintelligently as my brain processed the fact that my boss had flown here. "Mel, w-what are you doing here?" I asked.

He gave me a withering look. "I had no choice. You've ignored all my calls and texts for days. I thought you'd slipped off the side of a mountain or were eaten by a mountain lion. But it seems I was wrong."

He looked pointedly at Jacob, who I felt bristle beside me. I felt horrified. Mel was right. I'd been so caught up with Jacob and Christmas Mountain that I hadn't really given work a second thought. I'd even turned my phone off.

"Mel, I'm so sorry," I said, totally hoping I wasn't fired. My stomach knotted as I imagined my light and bright studio apartment evaporating before my eyes. "I know I said I was taking the weekend off, but I've been busy scouting for locations. And this mountain air—phew—it wipes me out, so as soon as I get back to my room then I'm practically falling asleep from exhaustion."

I was aware that I was rambling and so was Mel, because he held his gold-ringed hand up to silence me.

"That's not good enough, Lacey. Not good enough at all."

Mel looked furious. Fear rolled through me in hot, tumultuous waves. Suddenly, I was scared for my life. It's like I was drowning and I wanted a lifesaver, but none were within reach. Was I about to be fired? The look on Mel's face said yes. This was so *not* good.

CHAPTER SIXTEEN

There was an awkward silence at the bottom steps of the Falls and the only things that moved were the clouds of breath coming from Mel, Jacob and me. Actually, Mel's breath was coming and going a lot quicker than mine or Jacob's. I wasn't sure if it was from anger or the shock of finding himself in freezing temperatures. Let's hope for the latter.

Mel was a strictly 'sun, sea, and sand' man. I never imagined he'd come up here to find me in a million years. Doom and gloom seemed like looming prospects for my life right about now. I should say something, anything, that could resurrect my career but I was too stunned to speak.

Finally, Jacob coughed pointedly beside me, giving my arm a little nudge.

I jumped, popping out of my shell-shock.

"Introductions!" I blurted, as if I'd had a great idea. This. Was. Such. A. Debacle. I cleared my throat. "Jacob, this is my boss, Melvin Pennington. Mel, this is Jacob Curtis, tour guide extraordinaire from the Sugar Plum Inn where I'm staying."

"Nice to meet you." Jacob held out his hand to Mel.

As Jacob's hand hung in mid-air, an awkward silence ensued and I was pretty sure I heard a pine needle drop before Mel finally shook Jacob's hand.

"Tour guide?" Mel asked.

Jacob nodded. "Yes, sir. I've been showing Lacey around."

One of Mel's eyebrows shot up into his hairline. "I can see that."

For once, Jacob seemed at a loss for words. I suspected it had more to do with the fact that he didn't know what to make of this strange man from the city, but as the silence grew longer and longer, I knew I needed to step in.

"As you know from my reports, I've seen some amazing places, Mel. Christmas Mountain has many beautiful locations that will look great on camera."

Mel grunted. "That remains to be seen. No reports have come in for three days. What exactly did I send you up here for, Lacey? It wasn't for a vacation, a snowy sabbatical."

Jacob opened his mouth as if to say something, but I pressed his arm to stop him.

"Of course not, Mel," I said, quickly. "It was just the weekend and . . ." My eyes grew larger and larger as I watched Mel's brow crease further and further. Finally, I waved a hand dismissively. "Never mind all of that now that you're here. Even better than a report will be for you to see in person that this is the ideal location for next season."

Out of the corner of my eye, I saw Jacob cringe. I knew he worried that his town would be exploited for ratings, but I was thankful he didn't say his opinion right now.

"What would you like to see first, Mel?" I asked, forcing my voice to sound upbeat.

He made a noise, but then glanced to the top of the steps

at The Sharing Tree. "What's the deal with that tree? It's like a Christmas tree only a jumbled mess."

Jacob's jaw muscles tightened. "The Sharing Tree is a longstanding tradition in Christmas Mountain, Mel—"

Mel shot him a look.

"—vin, Melvin. The residents of the town and tourists come up here to hang ornaments at Christmas for the loved ones they've lost. By Christmas Eve the branches are completely filled; it's our way of including those who have passed on in our festivities."

"A tree to commemorate dead people? Not exactly what I'd call romantic." Mel's eyes rolled skyward. He began pacing in those cowboy boots, stroking his goatee with his right hand as he seemed to think. "Still, it *is* an interesting tree."

"It really is," I said, feeling Jacob's tension grow beside me.

"Here's what I need," Mel said, gruffly. "Write this down. Are you writing this down, Lacey? Write this down."

Mel always repeated himself when he got his teeth stuck into an idea, so I scrambled for my phone and opened the note-taking app.

"Ready," I said.

Mel held up a leather-gloved index finger. "There's a place I saw near the church, an open space—"

"The town square?" Jacob asked.

"The town square," Mel said, firmly, as if he had thought of it himself. "That's where the tree should be. Lacey, it needs to be moved there. And quickly, I have the crew on standby to come up here to start filming."

I tapped into my phone, my pulse racing as I processed what Mel was saying. He was approving the location. I was going to get my bonus. The apartment of my dreams. I was starting to feel a little faint.

"That thing will have to be moved as well, of course, that other ... *thing*." He snapped his fingers repeatedly, wanting one of us to fill in the proper name for the 'thing.'

"Kissing Bench," Jacob said, in a deadpan manner.

"Kissing Bench will be moved to the town square and set up next to the tree," Mel said, in a commanding way as if he were making a formal announcement. "Got all that, Lacey?"

I bit my lip, not wanting to deliver bad news. "There's already a Christmas tree in the town square."

Mel gave Jacob a look that said he'd messed up big time and Mel was not happy about that fact. "There is an empty space near the church with *no* tree."

"The bandstand?" Jacob asked.

"The bandstand," Mel said, waving his hand as if he couldn't care less about what the area was called. "The tree and the bench will be moved by the bandstand. We need wardrobe to bring costumes. Lots of plaid and flannel, very lumberjack-y."

"Plaid, flannel, lumberjack-y," I repeated, glancing at Jacob out of the corner of my eye.

Jacob's jaw muscle was twitching now. His hands were flexing, too. Not a good sign.

"Red sweaters!" Mel declared, clapping his hands together. "With reindeer on them and Santa Claus. It's Christmas, after all. Can you manage that, Lacey?"

"Red sweaters, reindeer, Santa Claus," I repeated, thinking this was all starting to sound a little too staged. My mind raced, trying to find the right way to explain this to him.

"To the bandstand," Mel said, heading down the sidewalk.

A Sugar Plum Christmas

I followed with quick steps, hoping Mel's cowboy boots had some kind of traction on the bottom for the fast pace he was keeping.

Jacob trailed along behind, looking totally bewildered by this overbearing whirlwind of a man who had descended on his beautiful little town.

He glanced at me, a line between his eyebrows.

Jacob had worried about his town being exploited for ratings and now I was starting to feel like the biggest hypocrite ever because it seemed like that was exactly what was happening. I had to say something, anything.

"Um, Mel?" I said.

He glared at the tree as we passed the town square, as if it had done something wrong by existing. Um, hello? The tree lighting was a town tradition. I'd hoped to include that in the show.

"Mel?" I repeated.

He stopped at the bandstand and held both of his hands up to create a 'photo frame' as he surveyed the area. "What?"

I was used to his abrupt ways, especially when he was in the throes of his 'creative genius' as he liked to call it, but Jacob looked appalled.

"Sorry," I mouthed to Jacob, who gave me a look I couldn't read. Sigh. "Um, Mel? You need to slow down a bit. Can we go back to The Sharing Tree?"

Mel turned in the opposite direction from where we had come. "Go back? No. Why should we? I've seen it, and I'm not risking life nor limb to hike up there."

I blew out my cheeks in exasperation. "No, I meant figuratively. Mel, stop!"

Most people were scared of Mel and wouldn't dare interrupt him, but I knew from experience that when he was spinning like this, he had to be reined in. It did the trick, and he stopped walking and looked at me.

"What is so important?" he asked, in a tone that indicated I didn't have to shout.

I held up my phone to look at my notes. "You said something about the tree moving to the bandstand, which seems . . . out of place for the tradition. Can you explain why we would go to such extremes? Just so I can, er, share your vision?"

"You need to fill in the blanks, Lacey. The Caring Tree—"

"Sharing," Jacob said, his voice thick with emotion. "It's called The Sharing Tree."

Mel looked at him as if seeing him for the first time.

"Caring *sounds* better," he said, as if he were explaining a simple math problem to a grade schooler. He walked around Jacob, appraising him from all angles. "You should submit to be a contestant for the show. You ever think of growing a beard?"

Jacob stared at Mel blankly.

Never have I wanted to plant my face in my palm so badly.

"Can we move on with show specifics?" I suggested.

Mel took a deep breath. "Right, here's what I want. The Caring Tree will be relocated, costumes are started, a couple of local contestants sprinkled in . . ."

"Mel, we can't relocate the tree," I said, finally putting my foot down. "The Caring Tree . . ." I cringed, reassuring myself it was my job to call the tree by the name my boss wanted. "It's a beloved tradition in Christmas Mountain. It's a real tree, planted firmly in the ground. As far as the character sweaters, we might want to rethink them as we don't want to seem too staged, right?"

"Mere details." Mel dismissed my concerns with a wave of his hand.

"Still, something to consider," I said, wanting to steer Mel in the right direction without causing him to lose interest in this location because, hello? Big bonus!

"What's that? That wooden thing? On the ground. What's that?" Mel asked, repeating himself as he pointed to the sled that Jacob and I had been riding earlier.

"It's a sled," I said.

"Lemme see." Mel snapped his fingers and held out his hand, and I quickly hurried over to grab it and haul it back.

"Here you go." I held it up for Mel, worried that if Jacob helped then he might accidentally drop it on Mel's foot. I know that I kind of wanted to do it myself.

"This is charming, very small town. Where do I get more?"

"From me. I make them to order," Jacob said, sounding less annoyed for the first time since Mel arrived.

"Perfect! Get me twenty-four by the end of the week."

"Hold up." Jacob raked a hand through his hair. "You can't get twenty-four of these sleds that quickly. They're hand-crafted, not cheap knock-offs."

Mel studied Jacob for a moment, and then shrugged. "Lacey, take this down. Go online and find me the quickest way to get two dozen sleds by Friday. Drop my name, tell them they're for the show and they'll probably supply them free of charge."

I looked at Jacob, who pursed his mouth like he'd swallowed something sour.

"Mel, I think part of the charm of filming in Christmas Mountain is the hand-crafted, small-town, no rushing feel. Exactly as it is. This . . ." I swept my arm to gesture all around us. "This is what the viewers will love."

Mel stared at me, his cigar hanging from his lip.

"The contestants won't be able to help but fall in love. This place is magical. It takes you under its spell. This will be our best season yet. The people, the scenery, the traditions . . . they're what makes Christmas Mountain so special. Not quick sleds and Santa sweaters."

Mel studied me for a moment. "Lacey, you've been in the business long enough to know it's all about the ratings. And I have been in the business longer, which means I know what causes the ratings to rise and fall. And when ratings fall, so do staffing levels."

Jacob blew out an audible breath and took a step back.

I stood still, not knowing what to do. If I walked away with Jacob, my job would be on the line, but if I went along with Mel's plans, I felt like I'd be betraying Jacob.

Mel noticed my hesitation and narrowed his eyes. "You know, if this season pulls in the viewers the way I think it will, you're in for a huge promotion in addition to your bonus, Lacey. After all, you found the place so its success will rest on your shoulders."

I stood between Jacob and Mel. Both men were silent, and both of them looked at me expectantly. Then I realized there was no choice to make. I was here to do a job. I'd never promised Jacob anything regarding filming. Mel knew this business and took me on when I knew nothing. He'd never deserted me and I wasn't going to let him down.

"Okay, Mel," I said, unable to look Jacob in the eye. I pulled out my phone again, and opened up the note-taking app. "Start from the beginning on your vision."

As Mel began to talk, I turned to Jacob, hoping he would understand, but he was already out of earshot and striding toward the inn without me.

CHAPTER SEVENTEEN

I closed the door of the Sugar Plum Inn behind me and leaned back against it, letting out a big sigh. If I'd been in my actual room then I would've slid down the wood until I was sitting on the floor, and probably stayed there until morning.

The last few hours with Mel had exhausted me. Back in New York, B.C. (as in New York, Before Christmas Mountain), I had been used to this high speed and frenetic pace of *Fourteen Days Till Forever* and everything that went with it. But being here in Christmas Mountain had made me realize that life was so much more enjoyable for me when it went slower.

Mel had insisted on going everywhere in his giant Hummer, so we stood out like a sore thumb, making me cringe. His flamboyance was accepted and even celebrated in the city, but here I just felt embarrassed by his showiness. It felt like an act, a spectacle for onlookers, which didn't sit right in this community of lovely, down to earth people.

Some of the locations I wanted to show him were practically next to each other, but still he insisted on the car driving us those few blocks.

"I'm not ruining these boots, Lacey. And speaking of shoes . . ." He'd looked down at my feet which were still sporting Ruby's walking boots. "You might want to think about taking your styling up a notch once filming starts." He'd started laughing then. "Right now, all I can say is, you really look like you belong here."

I'd bitten my tongue to stop me saying, "I wish."

Finally, after hours of driving around, jumping in and out of the limo, and listening to Mel's heartbreaking plans to change things in this town—*we need to move the ice rink to Santa's Village, what do I care if the village is in a forest? Cut down some trees to make room for it*—I had a thumping headache and aching legs to boot.

I pushed away from the door and shrugged off my coat before bending to unlace the unstylish boots Mel disliked.

"Rough day?" came a familiar female voice.

"Ruby!" I jumped, nearly toppling over as I grappled with the laces, and stood up.

"I nearly had a heart attack. I didn't see you there."

She smiled. "That was the intention."

My face fell. "Have I done something to upset you?"

She shook her head. "Not hiding from you . . . just the world. I'm hiding from the world."

I nodded, moving over to the armchair to sit near Ruby. I held my hands up to warm them in front of the fire. "I can relate to that."

"So, I was right? It *was* a rough day?" she asked.

"You could say that," I said, leaning my head against the back of the chair, which (on the bright side) was more comfortable than the front door. "My boss, Mel, is in town."

That last sentence should have been followed by a dramatic *dun-dun-dunnn*, because Mel invited drama wherever he went.

Ruby reached across the coffee table and lifted a tea pot, holding it up to ask if I wanted any.

I nodded. "I'd love a cup, thanks."

Ruby stood up and collected a clean mug from the cabinet before filling the hot liquid to the top and then sliding the spicy scented deliciousness across the table.

"You look how I feel," she said.

"I'm not sure that's a compliment," I joked, accepting the drink and holding it up to watch the firelight dancing. The first sip warmed my throat and all of my insides, soothing me like a comfy blanket. "Thank you, Ruby. I needed this."

"My pleasure," she said, giving me a half-smile.

Neither of us spoke for several minutes. I rested my sock-covered feet on the ottoman in front of me, and realized I felt at home here—not just at the inn but in this town. I'd even missed a call from Harmony from the book club, who'd left a cheery voicemail asking me how my day had gone. Thinking of my life in New York made me feel sad and kind of lonely that I had so many acquaintances but no real friends. Not until I'd come here, anyway.

"Tell me about your day, Ruby. Looks like it wasn't much better than mine."

"Oh, it's nothing," she said, frowning as she took a sip of her spicy tea. "No, that's not right. It's everything, actually. Ribbons is still missing and I have no idea where else to look."

I felt guilty. I'd been so wrapped up in my own problems that I'd completely forgotten about the AWOL St. Bernard.

"You weren't able to catch him when he ran off? Poor

Ribbons . . ." I trailed off as a stricken expression crossed Ruby's face. "I'm sure he's fine and being spoiled somewhere, but it's awful for you not knowing where he is. Let me help you find him, Rubes."

She shook her head, her face taking on a determined look. It was a look I knew well, because I'd seen it in the mirror many, many times.

"It's my fault he bolted, so it's up to me to find him."

I felt slightly irritated, no, *frustrated* with Ruby because I knew this stubbornness well, this independence and belief that you had to do everything yourself. It was something I had spent years cultivating, but mine had been born out of necessity.

"Ruby, you are literally surrounded by people who would love to help you look for Ribbons," I said gently, knowing personally how hard it would be for her to relinquish control.

"I know," she said quietly.

"So, let us help. We can set up a search party and each take a different area to look. Like you did with . . . what was his name, the reindeer that went missing?"

"Rudy," she replied, smiling at the memory.

"Right, Rudy. Everyone pitched in then, so let everyone pitch in and help with Ribbons. You look exhausted, and it must be worrying you terribly."

"It's not that simple," she said.

"Don't I know it." I gave a mirthless chuckle. "You're talking to the queen of independence and stubbornness. You can take that *surprised* look off your face, because it is merely stubbornness. But I get it, I really do."

I moved to the couch so I could sit next to her. I was going to take her hand but I wasn't sure how she'd feel about it, so I didn't. Instead, I sat at an angle facing her.

"Ruby, you have no idea how lucky you are to be surrounded by so many wonderful, loving people," I said, feeling a bit envious of her life. "It's not like that for me in New York."

Ruby sighed. "I've never been to New York."

"It's a great city. There's so much to do, so much culture and opportunities. But it's also fast and furious. It seems like life passes by in a blur and despite the fact that there are a gazillion people living there, it can be a very lonely place to be."

Her eyes widened. "You can't be lonely, Lacey. You have the whole reality show thing going on and loads of people around you all the time."

"I do have people around me, you're right. And I love my work. But the people I work with are co-workers, not my true friends, and they're not family. Ruby, I would do anything for what you have here. I bet you could walk down Main Street and ask any single person for help, and they would drop whatever they were doing and help you. Am I right?"

She grinned. There was no denying it.

"So? Let them in," I said, giving her an encouraging smile. "You don't have to handle every problem on your own. Believe me, it's tough being your own island and keeping people at a distance. I've done it my entire life, and it's exhausting and lonely."

"Don't you have family in New York?" she asked.

I paused, feeling unsure about how much to share with Ruby. I realized that if I was trying to help her open up and let people in, then I needed to do the same.

"I spent my life in and out of foster care," I blurted, since this was only the second time I had talked to someone—other than previous social workers—about my past. "Each time I was sent to a new house I was full of hope, believing that they would be my forever family. But they never were more than temporary housing. After every failed placement, I slowly but surely built a wall around my heart. I had to be independent and insular to survive."

"I'm sorry, Lacey. That sounds really hard."

"It left me feeling very lonely. But you . . ." I paused, this time putting my hand over hers, "have your forever family, and your forever friends, so let them in, let *us* in. Okay?"

Her eyes shimmered and then her mouth curved upward, her face lighting up like the sunshine coming through clouds. She threw her arms around me and hugged me, and after a moment of initial surprise, I hugged her back.

"Thanks, Lacey. I wish you didn't have to go back to New York. I'm going to miss you."

I felt my eyes prickle. Truthfully, after experiencing all of the love and support in Christmas Mountain, I didn't want to be on my own anymore. The thought of going back to New York and leaving all of these wonderful people behind was almost more than I could bear.

"I'm going to miss you, too, Ruby."

* * *

The climb up the stairs at the inn seemed to take forever and my legs felt like lead. I wasn't sure if that was because my legs were exhausted from running around with Mel, or whether my legs were reluctant to take me any closer to Jacob's workshop, which is where I needed to go. The last thing I'd seen of him was his retreating back as he left me with Mel, and judging by his determined strides he hadn't been happy.

I didn't have long left in Christmas Mountain, though, and I couldn't bear the thought of spending it on bad terms with Jacob. So, I forced myself to deal with the situation and up I climbed, getting closer and closer to the sound of sawing coming from behind his closed door.

Taking a deep breath, I knocked on the door. But there was no break in the industrious sounds coming from within. I worried that it didn't mean Jacob hadn't heard me, it's possible he had chosen to ignore me. I lifted my hand to knock again, but hesitated . . . if he *had* ignored me then knocking again would just annoy him further.

But what if he *hadn't* heard me after all, and wanted to talk to me as much as I wanted to talk to him? What if his leaving was him taking a step back and giving me the space to do my job? It was no wonder I didn't date much. It was more exhausting than a day with Mel!

Hearing a noise, I checked over my shoulder to see if Ruby might be coming up the stairs behind me, but the staircase was empty. Huh. Weird. I turned to knock again, only to come face to face with Jacob, my knuckles about half an inch from rapping on his very handsome nose.

"Oh um, hi," I said, attempting to smile nonchalantly, but it felt like more of a grimace.

"Hi," he said, his tone frosty.

Okay, so he was probably not just giving me space for the sake of my career. Good to know.

"I was just passing by and . . ."

The hint of a smile flickered at the end of his lips. "Just passing by? My door is at the top of a very narrow flight of stairs that lead only to me."

"Busted," I said, thinking going for humor had at least ended his frosty tone. "Maybe I like to climb narrow stairs just for the fun of it," I suggested.

"Do you?"

"Well, no," I said, because there was no getting around that fact. I finally shrugged. "I actually wanted to talk to you."

"What do you want to talk about?" he asked, stepping back and motioning me inside. He swept some books off the winged armchair, brushed off some wood shavings, and then took a seat on a stool which he pulled out from under his work bench.

I sat down, the wood burner providing a warm glow. I gestured to the work bench. "Another sled?"

He nodded. "I have a couple of commissions to get done by Christmas Eve, but I keep getting distracted," he said, his mouth curving upward, which made me smile too.

"Distracted, huh? By who?"

"By Ribbons. That poor dog is still mis—" The last part of his sentence was lost behind the pillow I threw at him playfully. He picked it up and tossed it back.

I hugged it to my chest, feeling the need for comfort. "I do feel bad for Ribbons. Ruby, Morgan, and Morgan's boyfriend, Dallas, went to look for him."

"I heard." Jacob stood and moved to the bench. "Come and help me?"

"Sure," I said, joining him at the work bench, feeling glad to have something to do.

He took my hands, put sandpaper beneath them and moved them slowly along the wood. "Always sand with the grain, never across it," he murmured, his mouth close to my ear.

"Okay . . ." I closed my eyes, savoring having him this close to me.

"You're doing good," he said, moving back a step and

A Sugar Plum Christmas

raking his hand through his hair. "Look, Lacey. I'm sorry about earlier. I shouldn't have left like that, but I was—"

"Frustrated?" I offered, feeling a little frustrated myself that he was no longer holding me, even if it had been just for the purposes of sanding.

"Yes. I was surprised you would let some guy talk to you like that."

I straightened. "He's not *some* guy, Jacob. He's my boss."

"I don't care if he's a king of Funwertdome. He shouldn't treat you that way."

My eyes widened. "The king of *where*?"

He shrugged. "It was a made-up place I used to write stories about when I was a kid. Look, the point is . . ."

"The point is that he is my boss, so I have no choice."

Jacob stared at me. "But you *do* have a choice about working for him."

I could feel myself getting annoyed, which was the exact opposite of how I wanted to feel. "So, what? You think I should quit my job? Be out of work? Give up everything I've worked so hard for?"

Jacob shrugged. "If that's what's needed."

I put my hand on my hip. "You do realize this is the real world, right? Not some made-up kingdom from when you were a boy?"

He frowned. "I live in the real world, Lacey."

"No, you don't," I said, the words sharp on my tongue. "You live in this perfect world with family and friends at this beautiful inn in this special town. You have no idea what it's like to fend for yourself in a huge city, always competing to keep my job. Because, let me tell you, one wrong move and there are a hundred other people willing to step into my shoes."

"Or furry boots," he mumbled.

"This is serious," I said, staring at him and wondering how he could make a joke right now. "I don't need you taking a swipe at how I dress or lecture me on my career. In the *real world*, people who care about you are supportive of your life choices. Those people stand by you and don't poke fun at fashionable footwear."

Jacob's mouth twitched.

He was laughing at me. My eyes burned and I made a dash for the door.

"Lacey, wait." He hurried to the door and put a gentle hand on my arm. "Please."

I watched him back toward the wood burner, begging with his eyes for me to follow. I felt the anger recede and the tiredness come back as I sank into the armchair, leaning my head against the winged side.

"I'm sorry," he said, handing me the blanket, which had been draped across the back of the chair. "I was just trying to lighten the mood."

I pulled the blanket up to my chin. "It's been a long day."

Jacob smoothed my hair, tucking a wisp behind my ear. "I'm not going to apologize for hating the way he speaks to you, but it's your life. I'm here for you, Lacey. I want you to know that I do support you. Okay?"

I nodded, not trusting myself to speak.

"It's been a long day for me, too." He moved from the stool onto the floor in front of me, slipped under the blanket and he clasped my hands in my lap. "I'm struggling, Lacey, knowing you'll be going back to New York soon. I don't want to imagine life without you here in Christmas Mountain."

"It's hard for me to think about, too," I admitted, looking into those earnest blue eyes.

He touched my cheek and when he moved toward me, I

leaned closer and closed my eyes as our lips met. It was the sweetest kiss I'd ever known. My heart ached with the thought that what had just started between us could soon be over. As he kissed me again, I felt like that lost little girl growing up hoping only to be let down again and again.

CHAPTER EIGHTEEN

After showing Mel my proposed shooting locations all week, I woke up on the day before Christmas Eve with an uneasy feeling in the pit of my stomach. Today was my penultimate day in Christmas Mountain. Tonight, I would be boarding the private jet with Mel to take us home to New York. The word "home" echoed through my mind several times.

Mel handed me a personally signed bonus check last night, which had prompted me to hug him. He seemed embarrassed by my display of appreciation but patted me on the back saying he knew I could do it. The compliment felt good. I'd called the real estate agent about the studio apartment that interested me and she said that it was still available. She scheduled a showing with me for the day after Christmas. My dream was finally becoming a reality.

So why wasn't I ecstatic?

After staying up late talking with Jacob, I had returned to my room and then tossed and turned all night. So many confusing dreams rolled through my mind. Jacob, the Sugar Plum Inn, The Mistletoe Book Club, and even Ribbons had made an appearance. Each dream, though, ended with me having to say goodbye.

Anxiety rolled through me as I forced myself out of bed and into the shower. I knew today would be all about Mel. Any day with my boss was challenging, but today was set to be *bone-crushingly* intense since I didn't even know what he had planned, and would have to wing it as we went. He'd sent me a text last night telling me I was required to be at the Christmas tree in the town square at noon and to be ready, which meant I had to be ready for anything.

When I got out of the shower, my stomach knotted and I felt in no mood for breakfast. I had a couple of hours before I needed to be at the town square, so I decided to pack most of my stuff. My eyes burned as I stuffed my clothes into my suitcase, not wanting to believe that by late tonight I would be back in New York.

This quaint little town had become my home away from home. I bit my bottom lip, knowing it was more than that. Christmas Mountain felt like my *actual* home. My heart ached to think that I had to say goodbye to this special town and its warm and welcoming people.

When I finally went downstairs, the dining room was empty. Some of the guests had checked out in order to get back home in time for Christmas, and the others must've eaten by now. Betty was nowhere to be seen. There was plenty of food left out and I knew I was always welcome to help myself to whatever was in the kitchen, but my appetite had deserted me. So, I grabbed a cup of coffee and made my way to the couch by the fire.

As I sat staring into the flames, the office door opened and Betty came out, dressed in a beautiful red coat with a fancy hat to match. She was even wearing lipstick.

"Got a hot date, Betty?" I asked, smiling.

She patted her hat and smiled. "As a matter of fact, yes. Your big movie producer announced that everyone should come to the town square at noon for an important announcement. I want to make sure I get a front row seat. Or a good standing space, at least. It's not every day we have a celebrity in town." She put her hand to her mouth, embarrassed. "Except you, dear, but you have already become part of the family."

My heart warmed. "Thanks, Betty. That means a lot. But don't be too impressed with Mel. He's not exactly Steven Spielberg."

Betty laughed. "Oh, goodness. I hope not. We don't want any of those dinosaurs running amuck in Christmas Mountain. We'd have to call them *Brookelanchasauruses*. Or would they be *Brookelanchasauri*? I never can tell how to pluralize animals correctly."

"No worries. I get your meaning." I laughed, wondering if Betty had hit the mulled wine before noon. A few moments later, my eyebrows came together. "So, when you say that Mel has called everyone to the town square, do you mean the whole town?"

She nodded, straightening her hat in the mirror over the fire. "Every last one of us was invited. There was even an announcement in The Christmas Mountain Herald. Apparently, he wants to 'consult' with us about his big announcement. Imagine that, a big star like that wanting to 'consult' with us townsfolk."

I frowned. I had never known Mel to consult with anyone over anything. We chatted for a few minutes and then Betty was out the door before I'd finished my coffee. I took a deep breath, knowing I was stalling. Usually I was early to my work appointments. But for some reason, I was dreading this one big time.

A Sugar Plum Christmas

At quarter to noon, I left the Sugar Plum Inn, pulling my coat tightly around me. Brrr. It was a cold one today. I walked down the street and as I got close to the Christmas tree my eyes widened at the sea of people standing before me. I didn't even know this many people lived in Christmas Mountain. There was a buzz of excitement in the air, and I could see that a big microphone had been set up in front of the tree. As I approached the tree, a hand touched my elbow and my heart soared, thinking it was Jacob. But when I turned, it was only Mel.

"You're cutting it close, Lacey," he said.

I blinked at him. "You said noon and it's only elev—"

"Where have all these people come from? I thought you said this was a small town? Never mind." He didn't wait for my answer as he stalked off toward the microphone.

I looked desperately for Jacob. I was surrounded by lovely people but he was the one I really wanted to see. I scanned the crowd but he was nowhere to be seen and my heart sank. I knew he was still annoyed about the grouchy way Mel speaks to me, and deep down I couldn't blame him. But I felt like I was stuck between sucking it up (which I'd grown very used to) and keeping my job, my *dream* job, or speaking up and getting canned. Not a hard choice.

"Lacey, hi! I was hoping you'd be here." Macy's slender frame was lost inside the padded snow jacket she had on, and her hair was tucked under the hood. "I'm supposed to be at work, but when we got this invitation I just *had* to come. Ooh, this is so exciting."

I couldn't help but smile at her energy, which had been infectious since the very first time I'd met her at the book club in Rudolph's Reads. Macy and the gang had made me feel so welcome. She gave me a quick hug and then I watched as she disappeared into the crowd.

I scanned the crowd again for Jacob. Still no sign of him.

"Hey," Ruby said, coming up to me and holding a leash in her hand that was attached to a big St. Bernard. "Look who I found thanks to all the help you talked me into accepting."

"Oh, that's wonderful, Ruby," I said, giving the mischievous dog a pat on the head. "Where did you find him?"

"I spotted him through the front window of Coraline's Victorian house. He was on the couch, Lacey. And those did not look like cheap couches."

"I didn't get to meet Coraline," I said, feeling like I missed out on something somehow.

"She owns a lot of real estate in Christmas Mountain, including most of Main Street. She's a real hoot, too. Always trekking off on some adventure. A couple years ago it was an African Safari and last year she visited the Egyptian pyramids."

"Sounds like she really lives her life," I said, wondering if I was really living my life.

"You okay?" she asked.

"Of course." I nodded, even though I felt far from all right. Everyone in this town had taken me in as one of their own. Ruby felt like the sister I'd never had and spending time with her at the inn every day almost made it feel like we were living together. Blinking away the tears that were threatening, I forced a smile. "I should find Mel."

"Well, good luck. I'll see you later before your flight," she said, calling to Ribbons who had pulled the leash out of her hand and had run off into the crowd.

"Lacey, are you okay?" Carol asked, putting a hand on my arm.

I turned, looked into her concerned eyes, and almost burst into tears. She had been my only real friend in New

York and it was through her that I'd found Christmas Mountain.

"I'm fine," I said, trying to make it sound true.

"Well, you just seem . . ."

"Totally fine. Nothing to worry about." Just my heart breaking from leaving this magical mountain town.

"Okay, if you're sure," she said, not looking entirely convinced. "Listen, I know you're heading off tonight but do you think you can come to the bookstore this afternoon and have a last cup of tea? One last impromptu meeting in-person? We'd love to have one last get together with you before you go home and we have all gotten you a little something to remember us by."

My eyes watered as I nodded. "Of course, I wouldn't miss it."

She smiled and gave me a hug. "It's been wonderful seeing you."

When she, too, had disappeared, I looked around again. It was almost noon and I really thought Jacob would be here to support me. He must have received the 'town invitation' by now. Apart from anything else, I couldn't imagine Betty not telling him about it. I spotted her at the front of the crowd and made my way over.

"Betty, you nabbed yourself a prime spot here."

She hugged me. "Of course. I have my camera here all ready. Are you okay, dear?" she asked, looking into my eyes with concern.

I nodded. "I'm just going to miss this place, and all of you."

She pulled me into a hug and then stood back, holding me at arm's length. "And we'll miss you, too, dear, all of us."

My eyes watered and I nodded. "Is . . . is Jacob here?"

She shook her head. "He's just finishing up with the

second interview for that company in New York. He says it's just a formality and they have already made him a job offer. Are you glad that he'll be joining you in the city?"

"I . . . er . . ." All kinds of emotions flickered through me and I was unable to form any words to communicate them. Guilt at taking Jacob away from his family. Excitement at the thought of him being in New York. Butterflies that this wonderful man wanted to be with me so much that he was willing to leave the town and the people he loved behind.

"Are you okay, dear?"

Boy, if I had a candy cane for every time somebody asked me that. "Fine," I managed to choke out.

A loud whistle screeched through the air as Mel turned the microphone on, and he grimaced before barking at one of the crew, "Sort out this feedback *now*."

On cue, a young man scurried over and turned a knob down, before handing the mic back to Mel and then moving to the side of the stage.

"Good afternoon, ladies and gentlemen. I'm Melvin Pennington and I'd like to thank you for coming here today for this meeting."

The crowd cheered between shouts of, "Good afternoon!"

"As I'm sure you know by now, we are going to put Christmas Mountain on the map by shooting the next season of *Fourteen Days Till Forever* right here in this little town." He paused, waiting for the applause, which was slow in coming but did trickle out.

There was an especially loud cheer from Addie Wilcox, who wiggled her fingers at me.

I gave her a smile, keeping my hands clasped together in front of me. I would even miss Addie Wilcox even though I'd only met her once. Sweet busybody Addie, who I'd run into that first day while she was headed to her hair appointment.

Mel coughed, and continued. "Of course, we will need to make a few changes around here in order to make this season more television friendly, which I'm sure you understand."

Murmurs rippled through the crowd. "What kind of changes?" Addie asked.

"Just a few subtle improvements to make things work for the camera."

I cringed. There was no way these people would call moving The Sharing Tree—or The Caring Tree, if you were talking to Mel—and replanting it beside the bandstand an improvement. I didn't blame them, either. Unlike so many places which had forfeited their charm for the sake of commercialism, Christmas Mountain had retained everything which made it charming.

"To tell you more about our proposal, please welcome the producer of *Fourteen Days Till Forever*, Lacey Lane."

I jumped as loud applause rang out with many cheers of "Lacey" coming from familiar and unfamiliar voices alike. I went up the steps and joined Mel at the mic, feeling a knot grow in the pit of my stomach. Why did Mel need me here when he hadn't filled me in on his plans?

He patted me on the back, something he *never* did, and as he did so he whispered, "They like you, Lacey. Just go along with whatever I say."

"Good afternoon, everyone," I said, speaking into the mic the young man had handed me. I smiled and waved at a few faces I recognized, blinded by the flash on Betty Curtis' camera. I still wanted Jacob here to support me, but when I remembered where he was a tsunami of emotions washed over me.

"We have some exciting changes to share with you and we'd love your feedback, because your support will be crucial to the success of the show."

A lump formed in my throat as I wondered about the long list of changes he wanted to make before the shoot. I noticed Carol looking at me and frowning in confusion, making me suddenly feel like an outsider in this town.

Mel took the mic. "First things first, we *love* the idea of The Sharing Tree, *very* romantic, *very* traditional. But..."

I closed my eyes and willed him not to say what I thought he was going to say.

"We are going to need to move the tree."

A stunned silence fell on the shocked crowd.

"It's impractical where it is currently located, and quite frankly it would be a nightmare to shoot up there. At the show's expense, we will bring in heavy plant machinery to dig it up."

A gasp went through the crowd.

I cringed.

"We will relocate the tree over there by the bandstand. *Much* more practical for filming and it's close to the coffee shops, so the crew can caffeinate up as we film. We could set up a small booth by the bandstand, to sell the show's t-shirts and it will work out much better."

Betty lowered her camera and looked from Mel to me, and then back again as if she couldn't believe her ears. Yeah, I knew how she felt.

"Speaking of coffee shops, we will be using the pancake house in quite a few scenes."

I caught sight of Lauren's eyes going wide.

"But we will need to do a refurb," he said, in a tone that said this obviously couldn't be helped. "The décor in there looks older than the mountain."

A Sugar Plum Christmas

I shook my head and covered my mouth with my hand, but not before seeing Lauren's devastated face. This. Was. A. Nightmare.

"We'll keep the chrome, but the red leather booths have got to go." He consulted his tablet for more notes, while I wished the earth to open up and swallow me. "Ah, yes, Snowflake Skating rink. This is a great name. We'll keep it," he said, as if he controlled that decision. "I know a company, a leading supplier of skates, who are amped to get involved, so we will pull down the wooden shacks and put a modern skate store in its place. At our expense, of course. Are you starting to understand the improvements and how they will benefit the town?"

I didn't dare look around for old Mr. Clauson, who had spent the past few decades making beautiful, hand-crafted skates in the 'shacks' by the rink. I could feel tension in my shoulders increasing with each suggestion he made, but this seemed like nothing compared to the shock rattling amongst the crowd. For the first time, I was glad that Jacob wasn't here to witness this atrocity.

"And I guess you'll be wanting to move the waterfall, too?" a sarcastic voice called out.

Mel's eyebrows came together, obviously confused as to what the problem could be. "Waterfall, waterfall . . . yes, here it is. Well, obviously, we can't move an *entire* waterfall, so we propose to build a man-made mini Christmas Falls that will mimic the real thing. This way the pool at the bottom can be heated and more user-friendly for the contestants. The mini Falls will be an investment on our part, which we will leave behind for all to enjoy at a very reasonable cost. We will use recorded waterfall sounds so it seems authentic, and then use some blurry shots of the fake one to add ambience."

The level of noise was rising and the tension in my shoulders was making my head ache.

"What you need to remember is how good this will be for the town." Mel tried to pacify the crowd, but it only seemed to make them more annoyed. "Let's hear what Lacey has to say. She'll reassure you that these are positive changes that you'll soon be embracing. Lacey..."

I had to talk after all that? Gulp.

"Yeah, let's hear from Lacey," Harmony called out, clapping her hands together.

Carol started clapping and a smattering of applause erupted from the crowd.

Feeling like the crowd didn't hate me (yet), which seemed like something that was about to change, I took a deep breath, knowing what I had to do.

"Good afternoon, everyone," I said, looking out at the crowd and seeing so many familiar faces. "First, I'd like to say that I've worked with Mel for three seasons of *Fourteen Days Till Forever*. He's a good man and an excellent executive producer."

"Thank you, Lacey," Mel said, giving the crowd a smile that said, 'See? Told you so.'

"He knows what would make this show successful businesswise," I said, knowing this was all true and that I wasn't lying. It would also be better if he stayed silent behind the scenes like he usually did. What was making him join me this time? I sighed and eyed the crowd, wanting to be honest with them and wanting to be honest with myself as well.

When I looked up again, there in the front row stood Jacob. His gaze met mine and my belly did a little somersault, quickly followed by an ache. Jacob wasn't wearing plaid or flannel. Instead, he wore his thick jacket and his navy-blue beanie, with that blond hair peeking out of the bottom. And he was here to support me, even though he didn't agree.

Thanks to Betty, I also knew that he was moving to New York so we could see where things would go between us. My eyes watered at the magnificent gesture. Wait, if Jacob was on his second interview and he already had an offer then why hadn't he told me about any of it?

"Lacey?" Mel said, giving me a stern look. "Tell the townspeople how the changes I'm suggesting are good for the show and for this town."

"Mel's right," I said, my brain trying to process why Jacob wouldn't tell me he was moving from this town he loved so dearly. He would never want to leave the people he loved, but he was doing it for me. I knew he was a small-town guy who would never leave Christmas Mountain for any other reason. "Mel's suggestions would be good for the show and would make the season successful," I said.

A murmur went through the crowd as people seemed to mull this over.

"Righty-o," Mel said, enthusiastically.

With the mic gripped in my hand, I stood on the bandstand and gazed out at the festive decorations of Main Street and the majestic mountain jutting up behind it. Something niggled at the back of my brain and my gaze shot to Jacob, who watched me with a solemn look on his face. The corners of his mouth curved upward and he nodded to me.

And then it clicked.

Jacob hadn't told me about the job offer because he didn't want me to lose my dream. There could be no other reason. My heart opened and then I knew. In this small special mountain town, I'd finally found my soulmate.

"Like I said, Mel's proposed changes would make the next season successful," I said, holding my finger up and turning in his direction. "But it's not the only way to make the show successful. There are many options."

"There are?" Mel said, checking his notes.

"The ideas are right up here, Mel," I said, pointing to my temple and the crowd chuckled. "For example, The Sharing Tree has been around forever, in its current location. Why not bring the viewers in to be a part of this beloved tradition?"

"I'm not sure what you're getting at," Mel said.

"We could make coffee-table sized replicas of The Sharing Tree," I said, thinking off the top of my head of what would've made me feel less alone these past years. "And we invite our fans to set one up in their home and hang ornaments each year in memory or in honor of loved ones. Or . . . in the hope and faith of finding a loved one, just like I did this year right up by the Falls."

The crowd rang out with murmurs and "Awwws."

"Mel mentioned Prancer's Pancake House. The décor is part of its charm, but the real heart of that restaurant is in the kitchen. We could film Lauren, making those delicious pancakes and putting a heart on just about everything to let each and every customer know they are cared for. Right, Lauren?" I asked.

Lauren nodded, and mouthed a *thank you*.

I turned back to Mel and noticed his face was turning an alarming shade of pink. I couldn't stop now, though.

"And the skating rink? Mr. Clauson has been making hand-crafted skates since before either of us was born. Visitors come from far and wide to buy them and to skate on the rink. Bringing in a big corporation would destroy that small-town charm."

"As far as the Falls, we could record small intimate scenes between contestants up there. Thus, the viewers will

A Sugar Plum Christmas

see what it's like to actually be in that spot. It's cozy and magical and filled with wonder and love."

"Viewers like pizazz, glamor, and glitz, Lacey. You know that's what brings in ratings."

I shook my head. "Viewers want to be inspired. You can reach them even better with truth and honesty in a special town like this."

Murmurs of agreement rippled through the crowd.

"Maybe we'd even bring in some new viewers who don't usually watch much TV," I said, winking at Jacob. I knew I was giving up the career I'd worked so hard for and my dream of having my own apartment, but maybe it was time for a new dream. "I've traveled to some amazing places, but for me nothing compares to Christmas Mountain. In fact, I'm staying here," I blurted.

Mel took a step closer to me. "How can you stay here? What about next season? You've worked so hard for this opportunity."

"I really have," I said, realizing I was having this conversation in public. But it seemed like everyone knew everyone's business in this small town, so why should I be any different? "I've been working hard, days, nights and weekends so I could finally have a place to call home. And guess what? I found that feeling of home here in Christmas Mountain."

A long silence ensued as Mel gaped at me, his mouth opening and closing like a big bass.

Then a single person starting clapping, the sound crackling out into the air and my gaze shot to Jacob, knowing he'd started it. My suspicions were confirmed when I saw his hands coming together. Soon, everyone joined in and the entire town was clapping and cheering.

"This is the home I've always wanted," I said, placing a

hand to my heart. "I've learned that the only security I need is being myself and surrounding myself with kindness."

"Welcome home, Lacey!" Betty called out above the applause and the cheering.

"I'm sorry, Mel," I said, handing the young man the mic and then moving to the front of the stage. Just like in the school auditorium, Jacob held his hands up and lifted me down and into his arms."

"You're staying?" he asked, his blue eyes glistening.

"I'm staying," I said, nodding.

"I just accepted a job in New York," he said, shaking his head. "I was going to tell you before your flight, city girl. I guess I need to call and let them know I'm not coming."

"I guess you do." I nodded, laughing. "Guess what else? There's something you don't know about me and that I didn't even know about myself."

"What's that?" he asked, pulling me close.

"I'm a small-town girl at heart," I said, lifting up on my tippy toes and planting a firm kiss on his lips. Jacob's mouth captured mine and warmth filled my heart.

"Ahem," came Mel's voice from behind me.

"Oh, Mel!" I exclaimed, jumping back a step. I'd almost forgotten I was still in a crowd.

"I take it this is the reason you're staying in Christmas Mountain," Mel said, gesturing to Jacob.

"No," I said, shaking my head adamantly.

"No?" Mel and Jacob said in unison.

I shook my head. "Everything in me knows that I belong here. That's why I'm staying. Jacob is just a bonus. A very big bonus."

"I remember giving you a very big bonus," Mel said, pointedly.

"I'm really sorry, Mel," I said, holding my hands up. "I

haven't cashed the check yet. It's in my suitcase at the inn and I'll give it back to you before you leave."

He shook his head. "I don't think so."

"Mel, I truly appreciate the opportunities you've given me. More than you know. You were the first person to believe in me. But it wouldn't be right to keep a bonus I didn't earn.

"You'll have to earn it then," he said, as if this were a no-brainer.

I gestured to the stage. "Didn't you hear me? I won't produce the show your way. I don't believe in it. The real and true small-town aspects are what feel right to me and that's the only way I would be willing to continue the work."

"I liked the ideas you mentioned on stage," Mel said, lighting up a cigar. "Why did it take you so long to speak up and tell me about them?"

"I-I . . ." Okay, now it was my turn to have my mouth opening and closing like a fish. "I guess I didn't want to disappoint you."

"Gotta be true to your vision," Mel said, blowing out a long breath of smoke. "If there's anything I've taught you it's that you must be true to your vision," he repeated.

"But what about you being true to your vision?" I asked.

"Are you kidding?" he asked, letting out a raucous chuckle. "I'm going to be on a yacht in Bermuda while you're filming this season."

My heartrate picked up as I realized what he seemed to be saying.

"And I can live here? Work on the show from here? What about next season?"

"One season at a time, Lacey. One season at a time," he said.

And with that, I threw my arms around him. "Thank you, Mel. You've always believed in me."

"Still do, kid," he said, nodding to Jacob and then to me. "Now that this is settled. I have a plane to catch. I'll expect a report in the morning, Lacey."

"Tomorrow is Christmas Eve," I protested, which felt like asking way too much in light of all he'd just conceded. "I'll have it to you the day after Christmas," I proposed.

"Not a day later." Mel's leather-gloved hand formed a gun and he fired it in my direction before he started walking away.

I turned to Jacob, who I noticed had been joined by his mom and Ruby. Mr. Curtis must be manning the desk at the inn. I fiddled with my hands. "I guess I'll be extending my stay at the inn," I said, looking at them.

"And you'll be joining us for dinner on Christmas Eve and Christmas Day," Betty said, as if the matter were settled.

"I would love that," I said.

Jacob held out his hand and I took it. Together, we all headed back to the Sugar Plum Inn.

* * *

On Christmas Day, I paced the thick red rug at the Sugar Plum Inn, feeling way too much anxiety considering I'd just had the most amazing turkey dinner ever with the most amazing people. I should be happy. Thrilled. Instead, my stomach bubbled with worry.

"The twenty-minute countdown begins until Mom and Dad start the TV production of The Nutcracker—a beloved Curtis tradition on Christmas that I'm glad you get to share with us," Jacob said, as he entered the living room area. "I call the spot on the loveseat next to you."

"Sounds good," I said, with a nod. I fingered the charm bracelet the ladies from the book club had given me the other day. They each had the same bracelet, which had a book charm and a mistletoe charm on it.

I started biting my fingernails as I quickened my pace back and forth in front of the tree.

"You're going to wear out the rug," Jacob said.

"Ha-ha," I said, wishing I could feel as calm as he did.

"Don't be nervous, Lacey," he said, stepping in my path and catching me in his arms. "Everything will work out. You'll see."

"How can you have such confidence?" I sagged against him and for about two seconds everything felt better. Then I shook my head, moved around him and started pacing again. "You don't know that it will work out, Jacob. You're just guessing."

He counted on his fingers and said, "The couple never put the townhome officially on the market. You're the only bidder. And you offered a fair price. See?"

"That doesn't make me feel one *iota* better," I said, shaking my head.

"Aw, honey, you speak Greek," he said.

"Only in dire circumstances," I said, throwing my hands out and stopping. "Why-oh-why hasn't Ruby returned with their response to my offer yet?"

"Maybe Ribbons got lost again?" he suggested.

I thrust my hands to my hips. "You are full of chuckles today, aren't you?"

"I just don't want you to worry," he said.

"How can I not?" I strode over to him. "This townhome is perfect for me. It's a two-bedroom unit, so I could use the second bedroom as an office. And it also has a small alcove where I could put my business desk if I decide to rent out the second room. Lots of options."

"True," he said, putting his hands on my elbows. "But still—"

"It's in a beautiful part of town and it's right next door to Ruby," I pointed out, my anxiety starting to kick up even higher. "If I need to borrow a cup of sugar, she's there. If she runs out of coffee beans, I can be there for her. Book club? Girls nights? A walk in the snow? We're right next door to each other."

Jacob scratched his head. "I'm starting to wonder where I fit in."

"Obviously not for calming me down," I said, deciding that pacing let out some tension so it was time to start moving again.

"Wait a minute. I have just the thing to calm you down," he said, holding up a finger and then disappearing from the room.

"Ghosted again," I said, shaking my head. "This time when I needed him the most."

Jacob returned carrying a large bouquet of poinsettias in a crystal vase with a red, green and white plaid ribbon tied around the neck in a bow. "Happy anniversary!"

"Oh!" I thrust a hand to my mouth and hurried over to him. "For me?"

He nodded, wearing a grin. "These are your two-week anniversary flowers."

"But we met sixteen days ago," I said, fingering one of the petals.

"So, I'm two days late," he said, shrugging. "I'll be sure to be on time for our one month and our one year and will always bring poinsettias, in honor of how we met."

I laughed. "You think it's romantic to keep remembering

that I knocked you into a pot of poinsettias?" I asked, giving him a goofy smile.

"In fact, I do," he said, setting the flowers on the coffee table. "Because that's when I first looked up into your eyes and knew you were my Nora."

"Jacob Curtis, you are the sweetest," I said, circling my arms around his neck and pressing my lips to his in a sweet soft kiss that made my legs turn to spaghetti.

"Ahem, you two," Mr. Curtis said, clearing his throat as he dropped down onto the sofa and picked up the remote control for the TV. "It's show time in T-minus seven minutes."

"Fresh cookies from the oven," Mrs. Curtis, said entering the living room area and setting a plate of oatmeal cookies on the coffee table next to my flowers. "What a beautiful bouquet! Who brought these?"

"I gave them to Lacey, since she knocked me into a pot of poinsettias," Jacob said, in a matter-of-fact tone.

"His ladder was way too far out in the sidewalk!" I protested, my eyes widening with horror. I adored Betty and Randall and did *not* want them to think I would knock their son into a pot just for the fun of it. My goodness.

"Sometimes things work out for the best, dear," Mrs. Curtis said, taking a seat on the sofa next to her husband.

Jacob shot me a look of triumph. "Mom thinks it worked out great that you knocked me into a pot of flowers."

"I said I was sorry multiple times, not that you ever accepted any of my apologies," I said, crossing my arms.

"I accept your apology, Lacey," he said, slipping an arm around my waist and gazing down at me in an adorable way.

"See? That wasn't so hard," I said, leaning my head against his chest and giving him a squeeze. Then my eye caught a framed photo on the mantel.

Sitting on the mantel—amidst dozens of framed family photos and photos of various guests—sat a photo of me from the other day on the bandstand stage holding a microphone. In the back of my mind, I remembered Betty's camera flashing just like a mom would do. "That's me," I blurted.

"We're proud of you, Lacey. It's impressive that you put together an entire TV show. I wouldn't have the first clue how to do something like that," Betty said.

"That means a lot," I said, putting a hand to my chest and covering my heart.

"I have news!" Ruby called out bursting through the front door, holding up the papers she held in her hand. "Who wants to hear the news?"

My heart pounded in my chest and Jacob instantly appeared at my side, his arm wrapped securely around my waist. "Did your neighbors respond to my offer?" I asked.

Ruby nodded, doing an air drum roll...

"Come on, sis," Jacob said, his tone urgent.

Mr. and Mrs. Curtis began doing lap drumrolls, building up the tension in my chest even further until I thought my heart might explode.

"Your offer on the two-bedroom, two-and-a-half-bath townhome has been . . . accepted!" Ruby said, handing me the signed contract. "You are now the proud owner of this townhome on Mistletoe Lane, pending inspection approval and all of that."

"They accepted? I have a home of my own?" I asked, my heart nearly leaping from my chest as my eyes watered and I gazed around the room at all of the happy faces staring back at me. "I have a home of my own."

"Congratulations," everyone said in unison.

"Now let's get the show started," Mr. Curtis said.

"Set it up, hon," Mrs. Curtis said.

"Oh, cookies!" Ruby said, popping an oatmeal cookie into her mouth.

Jacob led me to the corner of the room on the other side of the giant Christmas tree and turned to face me. "Are you happy, sweetheart?"

"Filled with joy," I said, smiling through my tears.

"You deserve it," he said, pulling me into his arms and then gesturing to something hanging above us.

"What the . . .?" I exclaimed, staring up at a giant mistletoe heart that resembled the one from my dreams. How was that possible? And here we were standing underneath it, too. "Where did that mistletoe heart come from?"

"Remember that night you fell asleep in my lap?" he asked.

I nodded. "Yep."

"You kept mumbling something about a mistletoe heart. It inspired me to make one and put it up," he said, caressing my cheek.

"I have a confession," I said, the corner of my mouth lifting. "I had been dreaming about you kissing me under a mistletoe heart."

"Well, then . . ." He smiled down at me. "It's time to make your dreams come true."

As I stared up into those beautiful blue eyes, he lowered his head and pressed his lips to mine. A warm feeling washed over me, the feeling of belonging and love as visions of sugar plums danced in my head.

The End

If you enjoyed spending time with these characters, be sure to read Macy's story in:

Fake Husband for Christmas
(Christmas Mountain Clean Romance, 9)

** To receive a FREE BOOK , sign up for Susan's Newsletter: susanhatler.com/newsletter **

ABOUT THE AUTHOR

SUSAN HATLER is a *New York Times* and *USA TODAY* bestselling author, who writes humorous and emotional women's fiction and young adult novels. Many of Susan's books have been translated into German, Spanish, French, and Italian. A natural optimist, she believes life is amazing, people are fascinating, and imagination is endless. She loves spending time with her characters and hopes you do, too.

** To receive a FREE BOOK, sign up for Susan's Newsletter: susanhatler.com/newsletter **

Facebook: facebook.com/authorsusanhatler
Instagram: instagram.com/susanhatler
Twitter: twitter.com/susanhatler
Website: susanhatler.com
Blog: susanhatler.com/category/susans-blog

TITLES BY SUSAN HATLER

Blue Moon Bay Series
The Second Chance Inn
The Sisterhood Promise
The Wishing Star
The Friendly Cottage
The Christmas Cabin
The Oopsie Island
The Wedding Boutique
The Holiday Shoppe

Christmas Mountain Romance Series
The Christmas Compromise
'Twas the Kiss Before Christmas
A Sugar Plum Christmas
Fake Husband for Christmas
The Christmas Competition
A Gingerbread Christmas

The Wedding Whisperer Series
The Wedding Charm
The Wedding Connection
My Wedding Date
The Wedding Bet
The Wedding Promise

TITLES BY SUSAN HATLER

Better Date than Never Series
Love at First Date
Truth or Date
My Last Blind Date
Save the Date
A Twist of Date
License to Date
Driven to Date
Up to Date
Déjà Date
Date and Dash

Do-Over Date Series
Million Dollar Date
The Double Date Disaster
The Date Next Door
Date to the Rescue
The Dashing Date
Once Upon a Date
The Island Date
One Fine Date
The Date Mistake
The Decadent Date

TITLES BY SUSAN HATLER

Montana Dreams Series
The Friendliest Festival
The Delightful Dinner
The Brightest Boutique
The Memorable Mountain
The Welcoming Wedding
The Happiest Hike
The Sweetest Surprise
The Comforting Christmas

Young Adult Novels
See Me
The Crush Dilemma
Shaken